'I seem to be forever saving you, Dr Pearce,' Jack said.

Kathryn swallowed, unable to break the hypnotic gaze. The kiss was soft yet sensuous and she closed her eyes, savouring the moment. Jack didn't increase the pressure and nipped her bottom lip between his teeth before running his tongue seductively over her upper lip. A shudder ripped through Kathryn's body and she felt herself begin to swoon.

He gave a hearty chuckle and her eyes snapped open. 'I didn't expect *that* to work so well.'

Kathryn wrenched herself free from his hold and stormed off. 'Of all the arrogant, chauvinistic remarks,' she mumbled to herself. 'How could I let myself be involved in anything that man does?'

Lucy Clark began writing romance in her early teens and immediately knew she'd found her 'calling' in life. After working as a secretary in a busy teaching hospital, she turned her hand to writing medical romance. She currently lives in Adelaide, Australia, and has the desire to travel the world with her husband. Lucy largely credits her writing success to the support of her husband, family and friends.

POTENTIAL DADDY

BY
LUCY CLARK

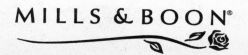

MILLS & BOON®

All the characters in this book have no existence outside the imagination of the author, and have no relation whatsoever to anyone bearing the same name or names. They are not even distantly inspired by any individual known or unknown to the author, and all the incidents are pure invention.

First published in Great Britain 1998
Harlequin Mills & Boon Limited,
Eton House, 18-24 Paradise Road, Richmond, Surrey TW9 1SR

© Lucy Clark 1998

ISBN 0 263 81282 0

Set in Times Roman 9½ on 10½ pt.
03-9901-62952-D

Printed and bound in Norway
by AIT Trondheim AS, Trondheim

CHAPTER ONE

'Look out!' Kathryn yelled as she hurtled down the icy slope. 'Coming through! Get out of the way!' She waved her arms about, the stocks dangling from her wrists as she tried to grab hold of them. Why, oh, why had she let her brother talk her into this? 'I knew I should have gone to Queensland,' she mumbled to herself as her frantic descent continued.

People in brightly coloured ski-suits were hurriedly swerving out of her way at the last moment. 'Look out!' she called again. 'Somebody help me—I can't stop!' Out of the corner of her eye she saw a dark shadow and quickly turned her head for a better look.

'Watch what you're doing and stop waving your arms,' a masculine voice ordered, and Kathryn obeyed. 'Snow plough,' he yelled, and she looked around for a large machine but failed to see one. 'Put your skis into a "V",' he called as he drew level. She had no idea what he was talking about but felt an enormous sense of relief as he stretched out an arm to her.

Kathryn knew she was moving too fast for him and wondered what he was planning to do. His speed increased and soon he was passing her. He swerved in front to cut her off, his arms outstretched to grab her.

Her body met his with a forceful thump and the arms that clamped around her thin waist were bands of solid muscle. She felt her knees go weak with relief and sagged against him. She was saved. Someone had saved her at last.

'Straighten your legs or we'll fall...' His warning came too late. She *was* falling for him—literally! As he toppled backwards his strong arms released Kathryn, propelling her into the air.

'Aagh!' It all seemed to happen in slow motion. One minute she was flying overhead and the next she was hurtling towards the whiteness of the ground at an alarming rate. Her body

5

crashed onto the hard, crunchy surface but her ride didn't end there. Sliding on her back, skied feet stuck high in the air, Kathryn did the only thing a normal, rational person would do in such a situation. She closed her eyes—*tight*.

A few seconds later she thought better of this plan and opened them, only to see the end of her current folly looming closer. An enormous rock. There was nothing she could do, nowhere she could go, except directly to her doom. She tried to make her body relax, knowing it would decrease her injuries, but her brain refused to receive the signal. 'Ugh!' she grunted as her head came into contact with the solid object.

Her eyes snapped open and she could have sworn she saw circling stars. A face loomed into view and the stars faded. His head was covered with a black ski cap, the colour of his eyes hidden by dark goggles. His nose and lips were smeared with white zinc cream.

'Are you conscious?' The lips moved, emitting a deep, resonant voice. He reached out a gloved hand to lift her goggles from her face 'Miss?' He looked down into eyes of honey brown.

Kathryn gazed up at him, unable to speak. She watched as he removed his own goggles and their eyes finally met. Warmth flooded through her as his blue eyes caressed her face. He was stunning, undoubtedly the most handsome man she'd ever seen, and here he was, tenderly running his hands over her body. She wondered, at his gentle touch, whether he felt the same pull of desire that seemed to envelop her. His next words made all her romantic notions float away with the breeze.

'Where are you hurt? It's all right, I'm a doctor.'

He was checking her out—medically not romantically. Kathryn closed her eyes in self-disgust. She felt him slowly remove her ski cap and then her long auburn hair was cascading down onto the white ground. He'd obviously removed his gloves because she could feel his warm fingers expertly explore her scalp before he cradled her head in his hands. Slowly his eyes travelled down to her full, sensuous lips, before returning to meet her gaze.

She saw the colour drain from his face as though he'd just

seen a ghost. What was wrong with her? Did she have blood on her face? Had she cracked her skull? Panic began to rise and with it came a blinding ache that pierced her head. Calm down, she told herself, but it was too late. The pain was here to stay. Deliberately, she raised her eyes to meet those of her rescuer.

'Jill?' He whispered the word in disbelief. 'Jill—is that you?' Once again he ran his fingers over her face, but the pain was too much for Kathryn and she allowed herself to be pulled into unconsciousness.

She roused to startling whiteness and for a moment thought she was floating towards the bright light at the end of the tunnel. She could hear movement but couldn't see anyone, and soon realised her eyes weren't open. An attempt to rectify this ended in frustration, coupled with a sharp, piercing pain that ripped through her head as she tried to move it. What was going on? Where was she and why was she so cold?

'On three,' she heard a deep voice say. 'One...two...three.' And with that final count she felt herself being lifted and placed onto some sort of stretcher.

'Ready when you are, Dr Holden,' she heard a woman say. 'The young lady was very fortunate you were around. And I'm fortunate to be seeing you again so soon. Are you sure you wouldn't like a permanent job here on the ski fields?'

'No, but thank you for offering.' His tone was polite but distracted as he focused on his patient. 'Let's get her up to the medical room at the ski lodge before she contracts hypothermia or any other complications.'

I'm all right, Kathryn tried to say, but found her senses not working correctly. She struggled to recall what had happened to put her in such a position but the forced concentration caused her to slip back into oblivion.

Her next conscious thought was to brush away the bright light someone was shining in her eyes.

'Lie still, please,' a deep voice said. His words were softly spoken yet with a hint of preoccupation. Kathryn's haziness began to clear as the light was thankfully removed from her eyes. She blinked, trying to focus, and finally met his gaze. 'Good to have you back.' He reached for her wrist and took her pulse, before noting it on the chart. Kathryn's wrist tingled from where he had touched her and she felt her colour rise.

'What...?' Her throat was exceedingly dry.

'What happened to you?' He asked the question for her and she blinked her eyelids in a 'yes' response. 'You were skiing out of control and I tried to stop you. Unfortunately, it didn't quite work out the way I'd planned and you careered into a rock. You've hit your head and fractured your left wrist. Your left ankle seems to have sustained only a slight sprain which, considering the way you landed on it after your brief stint of flying, is a miracle. I've just organised for you to be transferred to the nearest hospital where you can be X-rayed.'

He'd placed some chipped ice into a glass while he'd been speaking and now held a spoonful to her lips. She accepted it gratefully and tried to smile her appreciation.

'Have we...?' he trailed off and cleared his throat. 'Have we met before?'

Kathryn thought for a moment and took the opportunity to check him out a little closer. His body was firm and muscled—*that* much she remembered from her earlier encounter. His black ski clothes lent him an athletic appearance and she likened him to a panther—determined to get any prey he desired. His chin was square and strong and his nose had a bump in the middle as though it had been broken. His jet black hair curled slightly at the ends, indicating the need for a haircut.

However, it was his eyes that mesmerised her—the deepest blue she'd ever seen. Eyes she could continue looking into for the rest of her life. He cleared his throat again and Kathryn coloured at her frank appraisal of him.

'Ah-h...no.' Her voice was still a little hoarse but she continued, 'I think I'd remember if we'd met.' She swallowed convulsively and this time when she spoke it was a little clearer. 'I can't thank you enough for rescuing me, Dr...?'

'Holden. Jack Holden. Now it's your turn for identification. I'd like to get your particulars filled in before you decide to doze off again. Name?' he began, and Kathryn answered his questions. When he came to 'occupation' she smiled to herself, before answering.

'Doctor,' she said, and his eyes flicked up to meet hers.

'A doctor as well,' he said, with a hint of surprise, and for a second, Kathryn thought he was talking about something else. Jack shook his head. 'I've been trying to explain things as simply as I could when all the time you would have understood the medical terms. Are you simply a general practitioner or have you something more to confess, *Dr* Pearce?'

'I'm an orthopaedic surgeon.'

He raised his eyebrows in amazement. 'Perhaps I should call you *Mr* Pearce, then.' Jack chuckled at his own joke. 'Do you have a sub-specialty in orthopaedics? Dare I hope it's upper limb? That way you'll be able to help the staff at the hospital I'm sending you to.'

'Sorry,' she countered. 'I specialise in paediatrics.'

'Ah-h.' He tugged on his right ear lobe and look at her again. 'An orthopaedic paediatrician. And you say your name is Dr Kathryn Pearce?' He folded his arms across his chest and waited for her answer.

'That's correct.' Was it her imagination or had Jack visibly withdrawn from her?

'Well, Dr Pearce, as I said previously...' he looked down at the chart on which he'd been writing and made a few more notations '...you only have a minor concussion and all other neurological functions seem to be working perfectly. You have a left Colles' fracture and, I believe, a small tear to the left ankle ligament.'

There was a knock on the door and Kathryn had no time to reflect on his change in attitude before he'd started his 'technical' spiel of her injuries.

'Jack?' A long-legged brunette appeared in the doorway. She was dressed in jeans and woollen jumper but looked as though she'd stepped directly from a fashion magazine. 'How is everything going? Do you need any help?' The woman walked directly over to him and stood very close.

'I'm just getting ready to send Kathryn to the hospital for

X-rays. Kathryn...' he turned to face her '...this is Lyn. She's the RN assigned to this ski lodge.'

Lyn had obviously forgotten all about the patient lying in the bed, but she now turned and gave Kathryn a patronising smile. 'Oh, you poor dear. Skiing is extremely difficult for some and you really did make quite a sight, screaming your way down the slope. How fortunate that Jack was there to rescue you,' she said, and turned her attention back to the man in question. 'So strong and virile. However did you catch her?'

'I simply did what needed to be done,' he said. After making a final note on her chart, he handed it to Lyn.

'Some people are just born clumsy,' the brunette said matter-of-factly to Kathryn, but the warning that flashed dangerously in her deep green eyes was a signal women all over the world used when they wanted to lay claim to a man.

'Right, Dr Pearce. You're ready for transfer. I can't see any reason why I should come with you as you'll be able to tell them everything yourself.'

'*Dr* Pearce?' Lyn asked, her eyes wide with amazement, but she recovered quickly. 'I hope you're not as clumsy with your patients as you are on the ski slopes.'

Kathryn ignored the comment and gingerly turned her head in Jack's direction. 'Thank you...for everything, Jack. You've been my knight in shining armour.'

He gave her a brief nod and walked to the door. There he stopped and turned to face her. He opened his mouth to say something but closed it again, smiled and left.

Now what was all that about? Kathryn wondered. Once the door was shut behind him Lyn dropped all pretence at politeness and rounded on Kathryn.

'Don't get all cushy-cushy with him, you tramp. I saw the way you were looking at him. "My knight in shining armour",' she mimicked. 'You can keep your hands and your eyes off him. He comes here every season and during that time he's mine. I won't share. Do you understand?'

'All right,' Kathryn said defensively. 'I get the message.' She decided it would be better if she played down her reaction to Dr Holden, as far as Lyn was concerned. The last thing Kathryn needed right now was a cat fight—especially considering her present physical status. 'He was simply treating my injuries and being professional. You've got nothing to worry about, Lyn. I'll probably never see him again and, as it happens, I think I'll be leaving once I'm discharged from hospital. Skiing, as far as I'm concerned, is something I won't be trying again!'

Lyn seemed quite happy with Kathryn's reply and was more tolerant as she arranged for the transfer and paperwork.

'Hey, sis,' Steven called, waving his hand. Kathryn was thankful her brother was tall and therefore easy to spot across Adelaide's crowded airport arrivals lounge. She made her way to him and was instantly caught in a bear hug.

'How are ya, big sister?' he said, grinning down at her.

'Just fine, little brother.' She reached up and gave his arm a playful punch.

'How was the flight?' he asked as they made their way to the baggage carousel.

'Normal. At least from Melbourne it's only an hour and a half. Anything longer and I'd have been cramped,' Kathryn replied, stretching her arms above her head. 'I sincerely hope you didn't bring that motorbike of yours to pick me up because, I warn you, I've got a lot of luggage.'

'Some things never change,' Steven joked. 'Your arm looks good and you walked out here without assistance. Am I to assume everything has healed?'

Kathryn looked down at her arm. The plaster cast had only been removed a week ago. 'The wrist is fine but I still have my ankle firmly strapped, especially when I have a long stint in Theatre. Speaking of Theatre, are you up to your orthopaedic rotation yet?'

'Nearly. I've got four weeks left of my neurosurgery rotation and then it's orthopaedics. Which means I will be getting the chance to work alongside the most recently qualified orthopaedic paediatrician in Australia.'

Kathryn grinned. 'I still can't believe the training is finally over. Kathryn Pearce, M.B.,B.S., Fellow of the Royal Australasian College of Surgeons.'

'It certainly is quite an achievement.' He put his arm around her shoulders and gave her a squeeze. The baggage carousel had started to move and luggage was now littered along the conveyor belt. Kathryn pointed out which bags were hers and Steven lifted them off.

'Gosh, Kath. What on earth have you packed? Bricks?'

Kathryn laughed. 'Well, I am staying for six months. I hope you've cleaned the flat, ready for my arrival.'

He nodded. 'I don't know why I bothered. Once you litter all this junk around...' he gestured to her cases '...the place will be a mess again. Come on, let's get out of here.'

They spent a happy evening, catching up on family news and reliving some of their childhood memories. 'Remember that time when you and Jill decided to have a party while Mum and Dad were out?'

'Yes,' Kathryn groaned, and they both smiled. 'They were at a wedding on the other side of town and were supposed to spend the night with friends. But Dad got sick so they decided to come home.'

'That's the one,' Steven said as he began to chuckle. 'You're lucky Mum called ahead to let us know they'd changed their plans. I swear, I'd never seen you or Jill clean up so fast.'

'Mmm. I remember *you* refused to help because it was *our* party.'

'Well, you didn't let me invite any of my friends,' Steven protested.

'Steven, you were only ten. I was sixteen and Jill was almost twenty. It was very important for us to have that party but, gee, what a frantic time we had getting everything clean and ship-shape in just under an hour.'

'Did Mum and Dad ever find out about that party?'

'Yes. I told them a few years ago. It made them laugh and I think stories like that help us all to remember the good times we had with Jill.'

'I still miss her,' Steven said quietly, and Kathryn reached out to hold his hand.

'So do I, Stevie. So do I.' They sat quietly for a while before Kathryn yawned for what seemed the hundredth time. 'I guess

I'm more tired than I realised. I'll go to bed now and finish unpacking tomorrow after work. Thanks, Stevie.' She leaned over and kissed her brother. 'For everything.'

The following morning Kathryn was up bright and early. Unable to keep any food down because of a mild case of nerves, she waited impatiently while Steven drew her a map of the fastest route to the hospital. Although the apartment was close, she knew she'd have to get a car, but for today a brisk walk would do her good. Being on call for the emergency roster would mean all sorts of hours, and she didn't relish walking anywhere at night.

Arriving at the hospital, she found her way to the orthopaedic wards and introduced herself to the clinical nurse consultant who said, 'Call me Joan. We're all informal around here.' Kathryn judged Joan to be in her mid-fifties and immediately knew they'd be good friends.

She was introduced to some of the nursing staff who were at the desk and then shown where her office would be. She hung up her coat and put her bag down by the desk, before surveying the sterile little room.

'Before you know it,' Joan said with a chuckle, 'your desk is going to be piled high with case notes and memos and all sorts of things. Then, I'm sure, as Acting Director, you'll feel right at home.' They discussed a few more minor details, such as clerical support and research facilities, before Joan took her round to meet her superior.

'As you know, the director of orthopaedics is away for six months. His wife has terminal breast cancer,' Joan confided. 'All surgical departments are grouped together as this is a fairly small hospital and come under one main body—the department of surgery. Professor Holden, who also happens to be our chief neurosurgeon, is head of this department. He's been taking care of orthopaedics—on paper only—but now you're here, and our only permanent orthopaedic specialist on staff, I guess it's your job. You have five visiting medical orthopaedic specialists who hold public clinics here and are on the emergency rosters so at least you'll get a few nights off from being on call.' She came to a halt outside an office door, knocked and quickly opened it, without waiting for a response.

Kathryn followed her in and nearly passed out on the spot as she looked into Dr Jack Holden's blue eyes. *Professor* Holden, she corrected herself. *And* he was her superior. Her heart began to beat faster but she forced herself to take a step toward him. Her knees buckled and she almost fell. Joan was at her side instantly and offered support.

'Are you all right?'

'Yes.' Kathryn felt her colour rise. 'I'm fine, thank you.' Jack looked even more handsome than she remembered. His hair had been cut and a lock fell across his forehead, which he brushed back with impatient fingers. Kathryn tried to regain her composure and her balance as she faced the man who still reminded her of a panther.

Jack stood from behind his desk. 'Dr Pearce.' He nodded as they shook hands. Kathryn made sure the contact was brief and jerked her hand back as though burned. 'I see that your ankle is still giving you a bit of trouble. How's the wrist?'

She took a deep breath and squared her shoulders. 'It's fine. Thank you for your concern, Professor Holden.'

'You two know each other?' Joan grinned, looking from one to the other.

'Yes.' Professor Holden answered for both of them. 'Dr Pearce and I met on the ski slopes of Mount Bulla a few months ago where she sustained a few injuries from a fall.'

'Oh, my dear, you poor thing,' Joan commiserated. 'Had you skied before?'

'No.' Kathryn found she couldn't tear her eyes away from Jack, her brain ticking over as she recalled some of their conversation. 'And I doubt I shall ever go again.'

'Oh, come now, Dr Pearce,' the professor interjected. 'You mustn't let one bad experience colour your impression of the activity. Indeed, it can be very invigorating.'

Kathryn didn't miss the double meaning in his tone and replied carefully, 'I'm sure it is, but I've made up my mind, Professor Holden.'

'Will you two stop calling each other by your titles?' Joan

said in exasperation. 'You know as well as I do, Jack, that the children are decidedly put off by all this Professor and Doctor rubbish. Jack, this is Kathryn. Kathryn, this is Jack.'

'You knew I was coming here yet you didn't say a thing,' Kathryn said softly, and Jack raised an eyebrow. 'Placing me in this disadvantaged position.'

'You're very forthright with your opinions, Dr Pear— Kathryn,' he amended when Joan sent him an annoyed look.

'I usually always say what I think. I know it gets me into trouble most of the time but it's just the way I am.'

Jack's beeper sounded and he excused himself from the ladies. As he walked out of the room he threw casually over his shoulder, 'Welcome to the hospital.'

Of all the nerve, Kathryn thought. He hadn't even turned to face her, and his words hadn't sounded the least bit welcoming.

'OK, off to our next stop.' Joan interrupted her thoughts and ushered her out of his office. 'Down to hospital communications to get you on line.' Thankfully she didn't make any comment regarding what had just taken place. Kathryn's blood was still frantically pumping around her body in confusion at the man's effect on her.

Making a concentrated effort to do some deep breathing, Kathryn was back to normal by the time they entered the telephonist's room. The rest of the day passed without further incident or any more encounters with Professor Jack Holden.

That night, when she returned to the flat, Steven was sitting with his feet up watching television, obviously enjoying his days off. Kathryn stormed in and stood in front of the TV set. 'Why didn't you tell me that Professor Holden was the chief of neurosurgery at this hospital?'

'Well, hi, Kath. How was your day?' Steven said, and flicked the remote to turn the set off. He knew of old that when his sister had a bee in her bonnet nothing could be done until it was sorted out.

'Why didn't you tell me Professor Holden was the chief of neurosurgery at this hospital?' she repeated, and began pacing around the room.

'Would it have made any difference?'

'It would at least have prepared me for today, instead of making me look like a complete imbecile.'

Steven sat up and frowned at her. 'Do you mean you know him?' he asked incredulously.

'In a sense, yes. He was the doctor at the ski lodge who tried to stop me on my humiliating skiing mishap. He was also the doctor who checked me out and transferred me to the hospital. I told you his name was Dr Holden and yet you said nothing. How could you, Steven?'

'Don't blame me, Kath. How was I supposed to connect the two? I never saw him—you simply told me about him.'

'Didn't the way I described him give you any clues? Today was almost as humiliating as our first meeting. He was expecting to see me. He knew my name. He'd put two and two together and come up with four while I stood there like a dumbstruck idiot—at a complete loss.'

'Whoa. Time out,' Steven called, making the time-out signal with his hands. 'Cool it, sis.' He went over and put his arms around her, effectively stopping the flapping up and down of her hands. 'I'll say one thing, your temper hasn't diminished with age or experience.'

Kathryn could feel herself cooling down immediately. 'We can blame Mum for that. Jill and I definitely inherited her red hair and the temper to match.'

'Whew!' Steven wiped his forehead. 'Boy, am I glad I missed out. So what if Holden got the jump on you. There's nothing you can do about it now. Just be professional and do your job. The kids are the important ones, Kath. Don't ever lose sight of that.'

'You're right. As usual. How about a cup of coffee and I'll buy you dinner?'

'You're on,' Steven said, grinning.

Kathryn knocked on Jack's door and waited for his reply. When one didn't come she tentatively opened the door and poked her head around. He was sitting at his desk, concentrating on what he was writing. Kathryn cleared her throat and he looked up—startled to see someone there.

'Well, come in, Dr Pearce. Don't just stand in the doorway,' he said impatiently, and motioned her in. 'Sit down. I won't be a moment.' He turned his attention from her and continued to write. Kathryn did as she was asked, folding her arms across her chest.

It was the end of her first week at the hospital. She had a few questions, as well as requests, for the professor. Whether he would help her remained to be seen. She'd carefully avoided him where possible but knew it couldn't go on for ever. Strangely enough, it had been quite simple. When she'd realised the hold he would have over her department she'd thought they'd be crossing paths more often, but if the past week was any indication...

'I'm glad you dropped by, Kathryn. I was about to have you paged so you've saved me the trouble. Sorry to have thrown you in at the deep end but I've been away for most of the week, lecturing at the university.'

No wonder she hadn't seen him. She'd thought she'd done a good job of avoiding him. Easy to do when he's not even around, she chided herself.

'It's been a hectic week but I've enjoyed it,' she replied, and raised her chin defiantly.

'If you thought this past week was hectic, wait until I give you your complete workload.' He buzzed for his secretary. She entered within seconds and handed him a thick manila file. Jack nodded his thanks and soon they were alone again.

'This is the full list of your duties as Acting Director of the orthopaedic section. You will be required to attend weekly meetings held every Tuesday morning. The department meetings are held monthly and the hospital committee meetings are held bi-monthly. Registrar and intern teaching syllabus for orthopaedics is your responsibility, and the rotation changes in three weeks time. I've enclosed copies of the current teaching programmes for you to look at but, considering you'll be the one setting their exam, include what you think is necessary.

'You've already had your initiation into the clinics and operating lists so there's no need to go over them. This file also has a list of the reports I'll need at every weekly meeting, statistics, and so on, as well as details for the other meetings. If you require any other information or need to discuss confidential situations with me, my door is always open. If you can't find me my secretary always knows where I am and can page me when necessary. Now, do you have any questions?'

Kathryn sat there, stunned. Not because of the workload. No, she'd known when she'd accepted this six-month temporary position of Acting Director that it would be a lot of work, and she knew she could do it. She was stunned because Jack had spoken his entire spiel in a monotonous tone, as though he was bored with the whole thing and had said it all a dozen times. His eyes had been focused on the wall just to the left of her, and if there was one thing Kathryn couldn't stand it was people not looking her in the eye when they spoke.

'No questions, Jack, but I do have a few requests. The first is that whenever you are speaking to me in the future it's OK for you to look me in the eye,' she said directly. 'I don't appreciate people not making eye contact because it is disconcerting, not to mention bad mannered and rude. If you do it again, regardless of where we are or who is around, I *will* point it out.' She spoke calmly and quietly.

He acknowledged her words with a brief nod and deliberately made eye contact as he asked, 'And your next request is?'

'Clerical support. I understand the secretary assigned to the orthopaedic director has gone on maternity leave for twelve months. Do you plan on reappointing someone?'

'Yes. I thought that had been arranged. Just a moment.' He buzzed his secretary again and a few moments later she entered. 'Hazel, what's the situation with the orthopaedic secretary?'

'The hospital clerical department has promised to send someone up as soon as possible. Unfortunately, that may not be for some weeks. All of the paperwork is in the file.' She pointed to the one she'd brought in earlier, which was open in the centre of Jack's desk. 'In the meantime, Dr Pearce, I'd be glad to help when I can.'

'Thank you.'

'Anything else?'

'Yes. The teaching syllabus. Do I need approval from you? I

ask because you may think my methods slightly unorthodox, but they worked well for me and I'd like to pass on the skills—' She broke off as her pager sounded. Glancing down, she noted the number was that of the casualty department.

'Cas?' he asked and she nodded. 'Do whatever you think is best. So long as they learn the work and don't disrupt the running of this department, I don't care what methods you use.'

'Fine. I'd better go.' She accepted the thick file from him and stood up. 'Thank you for your input.'

She was at the door when he called her name. 'Would you mind giving Hazel your current address and phone number?'

'Why? Are you planning on sending me flowers, Professor?' She couldn't resist teasing him and he coloured at the implication.

'Ah, no. I need to have all my staff's details in case of an emergency.'

'I see.' Kathryn's smile broadened. 'I've already done it, Jack, so I'll expect the flowers at the beginning of next week,' she said, and turned on her heel to leave.

CHAPTER TWO

ARRIVING in Casualty, the smile was immediately wiped off her face as she heard the wail of children in pain. Sometimes Kathryn thought she made an awful doctor because she got too involved with her patients but as Steven had pointed out to her on many occasions, 'It's your caring and compassionate heart that *makes* you so fantastic.'

Now she was faced with another heart-wrenching scene. A little girl, who was still just a toddler, was sobbing into her father's shoulder as he cradled her in his arms. Kathryn walked over to the casualty sister to ask about the case.

'A displaced fracture to the femur. Her X-rays have just come back so if you'd like to examine her...'

'But *her* leg isn't broken,' Kathryn stated as she pointed to the child the man held.

'No, but her heart is, poor lamb. It's her twin sister's leg that's broken. Don't you think it's amazing the way twins can feel each other's emotions?' She handed Kathryn the chart.

'It says here she fell down the stairs inside the house.' She pulled out an X-ray and held it up to the light to take a look. 'Looks as though she'll need traction. I see she's been given analgesics so, if you could organise a theatre for me, I'd like to get her fixed up as soon as possible. Preferably within a few hours. In the meantime, she can be admitted.'

'Right away.' The sister nodded.

'Who initially saw her? I can't read this signature properly.' Kathryn shook her head in annoyance and made a mental note to speak to the casualty intern in question.

The sister peered over her shoulder and looked at the signature. 'That looks like one of Dr Sommerville's scrawls. He's with another patient as we're a bit short-staffed.'

'Fine,' Kathryn sighed. Overworked interns seemed to be in

all hospitals, in all states, in all countries. 'Don't bother him, then, I'll take it from here.'

The sister accompanied Kathryn over to the waiting family. Behind the father was the mother, sitting on a chair and very carefully cradling an identical-looking little girl. The only difference was that this little girl wasn't crying at all—yet she was the one with the broken leg.

Kathryn glanced down at the chart to read her patient's name—Prudence Florington—before saying cheerfully, 'Hello, I'm Dr Kathryn Pearce. And who have we here?' She crouched next to the chair so she was at eye level with the child. 'What's your name?'

There was silence as the little girl looked Kathryn over, before turning her face toward her mother.

'This is Prudence and her sympathetic sister is Penelope,' her mother said.

'That's a very pretty name, Prudence. I've got some pictures here of the inside of your leg. Would you like to see them?' Without waiting for a reply, Kathryn hooked the X-rays onto the viewing machine attached to the wall and flicked the switch. Light illuminated the dark radiographic film and everyone's attention was drawn to it—including Penelope's. The sudden silence was almost deafening.

'Look, Prudence, this is the inside of your leg. See how the pieces of bone don't match up? Well, that's what happened when you fell, but don't worry because I'm going to fix it for you and make it all better.' She switched off the machine and Penelope started to cry again.

'That's a lot of noise for one little girl to make,' a deep masculine voice said, and everyone turned to see who was speaking. 'Hello, my name is Dr Jack and I couldn't help wondering if there was a need for some very special medicine in here.' He gave Kathryn a wink, before walking over to Penelope and her father.

'I've got something very special in my pocket. Would you like to reach in and see what it is?'

Well, Kathryn would say one thing for him—he'd certainly captured Penelope's attention and she'd stopped crying. The little girl shook her head. No, she didn't want to see what was in his pocket so, while his eyes never left her tear-stained face, he pulled out a tatty old puppet of a dog.

'This is my best friend, Ruffles. Do you like him?' Penelope nodded and he continued, 'Ruffles is very good at making little girls feel all better because he always carries lollypops. Now, I wonder if he's brought any with him today? Would you like to look in my other pocket to check?' he asked Penelope again and this time she nodded. Reaching out a chubby little hand, she slid it into the pocket of his jacket and pulled out two red lollypops.

'One for 'Nelope an' one for P'udence,' she said, and held one out to her sister.

Mrs Florington reached out and took the lolly from Penelope's chubby hand. 'I don't think Prudence should have this right now so Mummy will keep it for her for later.'

Kathryn looked at Prudence and said softly, 'I need to have a little look at your leg and then I'm going to give you something that will make you go to sleep while I fix it and make it better.' It would have been easier for her to examine Prudence on the bed but Kathryn decided it would only upset the child further to be moved from the safety of her mother's arms.

'I'm sorry to have Penelope in here but every time we take her out Prudence begins to cry. I don't want to upset her any more than necessary in case she does some more damage,' Mrs Florington said softly.

'It's fine. Don't worry about it. I've organised for Prudence to be transferred to the ward and then we'll take her to Theatre. I'll come up to the ward with you now and explain the procedure to you and your husband.'

'Thank you, Dr Pearce.'

'Please, call me Kathryn. We try to keep things as informal as possible in this hospital because it relaxes the children.'

'All right—Kathryn. I'm Sally and my husband is Gregory.'

'Well, now that the introductions are out of the way, let's get Prudence to her special room. I'll just organise an orderly for you.' Kathryn stood and made a quick notation on the chart before she turned to leave. Unfortunately, she'd temporarily forgotten about the crowd blocking her exit. She stood for a moment to observe Jack as he made little Penelope laugh with his puppet.

Here he was—the chief of neurosurgery taking time out from his busy schedule to cheer up and entertain a child. She'd been told he was fabulous with children but this was her first opportunity to really see him in action. Even Prudence had managed a smile.

'Sorry to break up this party,' she said as she moved toward them, 'but I must see an orderly about transferring Prudence to the ward.'

'Great!' Ruffles the dog said. 'You're going to love the ward. It's so much fun. Can I come up there with them? Please, please, please?' the dog pleaded with Kathryn, and she smiled at Jack's hand-puppet.

'Yes, Ruffles, you can come too but only if you behave yourself,' she warned sternly, although the smile on her face belied her words. 'Penelope, can you make sure Ruffles behaves himself?'

'Yes,' the little girl said, and reached out a hand to pat the puppet.

'Good. I'll see you all up there.' She nudged past Jack, being extremely careful not to touch him, and went to speak to an orderly. He might be wonderful for the children but when he'd walked into the little room Kathryn's heart had done a flip-flop—and she wasn't quite sure why. She'd only left his office fifteen minutes before he'd shown up in Casualty so what was wrong with her?

Pushing the thought out of her mind, she arranged the necessary details for the transfer, then went to her office to collect a teaching chart that described all sorts of fractures so she could adequately explain the procedure to Prudence's parents.

She found them settled in a small private room, with Jack amusing the girls with his puppet. The twins were both sitting on the bed, Prudence propped up amongst the pillows while Penelope sat on the edge with her legs dangling over—a very precarious position which her father was monitoring closely.

'Sorry to interrupt the puppet show but I'd like to explain the procedure to you,' Kathryn said, after watching Jack for a moment. His face was animated with laughter that caused his eyes to sparkle. He was really enjoying himself and it brought a smile to Kathryn's lips.

'Use the treatment room across the hallway and I'll keep entertaining the girls,' Jack said quietly as he picked Penelope up off the bed and placed her on a chair, before continuing with his routine. Kathryn indicated the room to the Floringtons before she gathered up Prudence's X-rays and her teaching aids.

'Well,' she said, hooking the X-rays onto the view screen, 'Prudence has what we call a displaced fracture. You can see here on the X-ray that the bone is completely broken in two and the lower half of the femur—that's her thigh bone—is at least a few centimetres to the left of where it should be.'

Kathryn opened her chart and showed them a similar diagram. 'A displaced fracture means what it says. The fracture has displaced the bone from its normal alignment and we need to slide it back into place. The bone ends must be kept a few millimetres apart so that callus—or new bone—can form and heal the fracture. To keep the bones apart, Prudence will need to be in traction for approximately six weeks.'

Sally gasped and Gregory put his arm around his wife. 'How do you put the leg in traction?' he asked. 'Will she have to stay in hospital?'

'Yes. She'll need to be an inpatient for the treatment to be successful.'

Kathryn flipped her chart to a different page which displayed a picture of the thigh bone, knee and shin bone. 'Under a general anaesthetic I'll be able to position the bone correctly. The type of traction I'll be using is called skin traction. We place a special bandage, what we call ''sticky'' bandage, around the base of the femur just above the knee. We support the whole leg in a splint, a canvas frame, to ensure it's kept as still as possible. Next we hook the bandage to the weights that will be controlled by pulleys on a frame erected above the bed.'

'Will she need a plaster cast on her leg?' Sally had recovered from her initial shock and was listening intently to everything Kathryn said.

'No. Once I've manipulated the bone back to where it should be, the muscles around the bone will hold it adequately in place.'

Everyone in the small room was silent and Kathryn closed her charts and gathered up the X-rays. 'Have a think about what I've said and write down any questions. I want you to understand what has to happen and why. The more you can comprehend and accept, the better your attitude will be with Prudence. It's imperative you both display a positive outlook when you're with her and Penelope. I'm not saying it's going to be easy but I'm here to help in any way I can—and that goes for the rest of the staff on this ward.'

'We appreciate that, Kathryn. One of our main concerns at the moment is the separation of the girls. They've never been apart and I'm not sure how it will affect them.'

'I noticed that in Casualty,' Kathryn said thoughtfully. 'Would you agree to having a social worker come to see you and the girls? Clara Lexington is her name and I can arrange for her to see you today before I take Prudence to Theatre.'

'Perhaps that would be best. We love the little darlings so much that any pain they suffer, whether it's physical or emotional, affects us too.'

'Of course it does,' Kathryn said, and placed a hand on Sally's shoulder. 'I'll contact Clara immediately but you have me paged if there's anything else I can do.'

'Thanks, Kathryn,' Gregory said again, and held out his hand in appreciation.

When they returned to the room, Jack was sitting in front of the girls, pulling a very funny face, while Ruffles tugged at his nose. Prudence and Penelope were squealing with laughter, as were four other children who were seated on the floor, looking adoringly up at the professor.

'He certainly has a way with children,' Sally remarked to Kathryn. 'Is he employed specifically to entertain?'

Kathryn choked on the question and tried to keep a straight face as she said, 'No. Jack is Professor of Neurosurgery and Head of the Department of Surgery.'

Sally gave her an incredulous look. 'He's the big cheese?'

'Got it in one.' Kathryn nodded and the two women shared a knowing grin.

'He's brilliant with children.'

'That he is,' Kathryn replied, and felt a warm glow of affection spread through her for Jack Holden.

The following day was Saturday and, thankfully, Kathryn wasn't on emergency call nor was she required at the hospital for any reason. It was her first day off and she was going to enjoy herself.

She climbed out of bed and went to the window. She lifted the curtain and was met with a brilliant ray of sunlight, peeping through the fluffy white clouds. The ground was wet but only in patches, indicating it had rained during the night.

'A perfect August day,' she said out loud. Within half an hour she was in her newly acquired Mazda 121, driving toward an archery park. She'd checked the *Yellow Pages*, made some calls to gauge availability and consulted her street directory. After leaving a note for Steven, she'd almost skipped to the car.

Archery was a sport her father had introduced her to at a young age, and she was hooked. She'd frozen her membership at the archery park in Melbourne as she was only in Adelaide for six months. Kathryn hoped, as she guided the car off the road and eased it gently onto the dirt track leading to the park's entrance, that she would find equal enjoyment from this one.

From her telephone enquiries she'd discovered that this park was set up in a similar way to a golf course. Here you didn't just stand in front of a painted bullseye target and shoot. There were different courses, depending on experience, and a map which guided you from one target to another. The owners had a large property, hence the one-hour drive from the city.

Kathryn had brought her own equipment with her and, after a friendly discussion with the owner, set off in search of the targets. The walk through the bush was exceedingly pleasant and she enjoyed the solitude. The knots she'd felt build within her all week began to ease as the tension flowed out of her.

She was on the ninth target, her bow taut and the arrow poised for flight, when the crack of a branch being broken startled her.

The arrow went flying through the air, passed the target and disappeared into the trees and scrub behind it.

Kathryn spun around, an angry scowl on her face. The scowl was quickly replaced with a look of disbelief.

'If that's your best shot,' Jack Holden drawled as he leant against a tree, one thumb hooked through the front pocket of his snug-fitting denim jeans, 'perhaps I'd better take you off the surgical roster until we get your eyes checked.'

'Jack!' she whispered, then cleared her throat. 'What are you doing here?'

He stepped away from the tree, his bow held in his hand and a quiver of arrows clipped to his jeans. He looked unbelievably gorgeous in denim with a black polo jumper. The image of the panther returned and Kathryn took a step back in defence.

'Now, let me think.' He raised a finger to his chin. 'Perhaps...' he took a step closer to her '...I'm about to go swimming.' He snapped his fingers. 'No pool. Well, perhaps I'm about to go bowling.' He shook his head as he advanced on her. 'No bowling ball. Perhaps,' he said with a grin on his face as he came to stand beside her, 'I'm tired of rescuing red-headed sirens from the snow fields and wanted some peace and quiet in the bush. Or perhaps I'm just out hunting...'

Kathryn backed away from him. He was dangerous in this joking mood. Dangerous in more ways than one. She felt herself physically drawn to him and knew, for the sake of self-preservation, she must put as much distance between them as possible.

Not looking where she was going, Kathryn stumbled over a small rock and would have fallen backwards had Jack not reached out an arm to catch her. She clutched at his shoulder, trying to steady herself, but only succeeded in being drawn closer to the warmth of his body.

'I seem to be forever saving you, Dr Pearce,' he said, his mouth only inches from hers.

Kathryn swallowed, unable to break the hypnotic gaze. The fresh smell of his aftershave teased her senses while his firm, muscled torso wreaked havoc with her equilibrium.

She watched, as though in slow motion, his head began its

descent toward her waiting lips. Her heart hammered against her ribs and she let out a small groan before his mouth was finally pressed against hers.

The kiss was soft yet sensuous and Kathryn closed her eyes, savouring the moment. Jack didn't increase the pressure and nipped her bottom lip between his teeth before running his tongue seductively over her upper lip. A shudder ripped through Kathryn's body and she felt herself begin to swoon.

He gave a hearty chuckle and her eyes snapped open. 'I didn't expect *that* to work so well.'

Kathryn wrenched herself free from his hold and stormed off in the direction her wayward arrow had flown. 'Of all the arrogant, chauvinistic remarks,' she mumbled to herself. 'How could I let myself be involved in anything that man does?' she continued, with her eyes glued to the ground, searching for the arrow.

'Don't mumble, Kathryn,' he said from directly behind her. She hadn't realised he'd followed her and she glanced over her shoulder to glare at him. He held up a hand in self-defence. 'I thought I'd help you look. After all, I am the one who distracted you.' He wiggled his eyebrows up and down, taunting her with the double meaning of his words.

Kathryn ignored his remark—or at least she tried to. She'd never seen Jack in a teasing mood and it was very endearing. She found her anger beginning to evaporate. It was impossible to stay mad at him.

'There it is,' he said, and bent to pick up the arrow. He held it out to her, but when she went to take it he pulled it back. 'Not yet. I feel like some company this morning and thought, considering we're doing the same course, we could continue together.'

'Is this a truce?' she asked, with mocking disbelief.

'Sort of,' he said. 'If you want the truth, I'd like to see just how good you are—when you actually hit the target, that is. Besides, I always enjoy beating my opponents.'

'You're on,' Kathryn agreed, and accepted the arrow. 'But only on the condition—'

'Why does there always have to be a condition where women are concerned?' he asked, throwing an arm up in exasperation.

'The condition,' she continued more pointedly, frowning at his interruption, 'is that we both begin scoring from here. After all, you could hardly call that last shot fair play.'

He seemed to be considering her offer and Kathryn, who wasn't the most patient person in the world, tapped her foot on the ground in agitation.

'Agreed,' he finally said, and put a line through his score card.

As they proceeded around the rest of the course Kathryn was wary of any tricks Jack might play to distract her, but he didn't. Conversation between targets was kept to the weather, the beautiful countryside and archery techniques. Neither, by unspoken mutual consent, mentioned the hospital at all.

At the last target Jack was ahead by fifty points. All Kathryn needed was a bullseye to equal his score. Any points she got after that would put her in front but, unfortunately, Jack's turn came after hers. The only way she could win was if Jack missed the target. The chances of that happening would be next to nothing unless... A grin formed on Kathryn's lips as she took her position to shoot.

Exhaling a breath, she concentrated hard and was successful in piercing the bullseye every time. Jack applauded her after he'd written down her score.

'Nice work, Kathryn. Now stand back and let the master finish you off.'

Kathryn bowed from the waist, making a sweeping gesture with her hand. He hooked the arrow into his bow and pulled back. This was one of the moments she'd most enjoyed over the past hour—seeing the way the muscles in his back were clearly defined beneath his thin jumper. She exhaled again but this time it was for a completely different reason.

Jack shot bullseyes in quick succession, and with one arrow left to go the scores were tied. Kathryn positioned herself a step away from him as he readied his bow. She watched as his eyes narrowed, focusing on the target—the concentration evident.

The moment he was about to let go of his arrow she stepped forward and blew softly in his ear. The arrow was released and sent hurtling towards the target, where it missed totally and skewered a mound of dirt nearby.

Jack whirled around on his heel and glared at her. 'That wasn't very nice, Kathryn.' The look in his eye made her begin to squirm. 'You do realise there's a penalty involved for interference.' He advanced towards her, just like a panther stalking his prey, and Kathryn quickly backed away until she felt the hard trunk of a tree behind her.

'Nowhere to run and nowhere to hide,' he chanted, flashing her a winning smile. 'Revenge is mine.' He closed in on her, placing one arm on either side of her head. She could duck underneath them and make a run up the path for the club house or she could use her self-defence lessons to get out of this situation, but the truth of the matter was that she didn't want to escape. Much to Kathryn's disgust, she found she liked being captured by the great hunter.

'So, what's the penalty for interference?' she asked, her voice husky. She licked her lips as his smile disappeared.

'Believe me, Kathryn, you'll like it. As will I.' His head swooped down to claim her lips and this time there were no soft, gentle caresses but a hungry, devouring passion. Kathryn welcomed the onslaught and allowed her hands to run up his chest. He groaned at her touch and leaned in closer, deepening the kiss.

His tongue probed her mouth, seeking and exploring. Kathryn reciprocated in kind, and after a few more electrifying moments Jack slowly pulled away and looked down into the smouldering depths of her honey brown eyes.

'You're more dangerous than I thought,' he growled, and took a step back from her. Kathryn tried hard to control her breathing, pleased at seeing Jack attempt the same feat.

'I think a drink is definitely in order...to celebrate our draw,' he explained when Kathryn opened her mouth to refuse. 'Come on,' he said. 'I promise I won't make any more passes.' He crossed his heart and gave her the Scout salute.

Kathryn gave a derisive laugh. 'You...a Scout? I find that very hard to believe.'

'I'll tell you all over a hot cappuccino.' They walked to the club house, left their bows and quivers at the door and sat down to relax.

CHAPTER THREE

OVER coffee, Jack was the perfect companion. He told Kathryn little anecdotes about his time in the Scouts and other adventures. She had tears running down her cheeks from laughing so hard.

'One day my brother and I decided to build a doll's house for my sister. We'd been doing carpentry at Scouts and thought we knew it all. Mum thought it a good idea as it would keep us out of mischief for a while.

'The only problem was our natural initiative skills. The house we lived in had wooden floorboards so Chris and I decided it was logical to anchor the frame directly to them. We were gluing and hammering and sawing and generally have the time of our lives. Rachael's room was a mess but it kept the three of us out of Mum's hair for a whole day.'

He took a sip of his coffee and Kathryn leaned forward in her chair. 'And?' she prompted.

'When Mum came in to tell us dinner was ready, well, it was not a pretty sight. We were up to painting at that stage so it was almost finished. Rachael, who is eight years younger than me and six years younger than Chris, was covered in paint.'

'How old was she at the time?'

'Four,' he grinned.

Kathryn let out a whistle. 'Your poor mother must have had a fit. A four-year-old covered in paint, and I'd be willing to bet that you and Chris weren't exactly clean, either.'

'No. The good news is that the doll's house stayed exactly where it was. When my parents sold the house to retire to the Gold Coast we did a few repairs on it, gave it a new coat of paint and left it there for the little girl who had fallen in love with the room for that specific reason.'

Kathryn grinned at him. 'You certainly had an eventful childhood. It sounds as though it was a happy one.'

'For the most part.' Jack nodded and looked at his watch. 'Unfortunately, I have to leave.' He drained his coffee-cup and stood.

Kathryn looked at her own watch and was surprised at how long they'd sat and talked. 'So do I. I promised my brother I'd go shopping with him this afternoon.'

'Younger or older?' Jack asked as he quickly signed the bill and walked her to the door.

'Younger.'

'So you're the eldest?'

'Yes,' Kathryn replied. It was too complicated to explain about Jill and, besides, neither of them had the time. If she wanted to rationalise it she was the eldest in her family, considering that Jill's father had been her mother's first husband.

Jack seemed to digest this information before they collected their things and walked to the car park.

'New car?' he asked when she stopped beside the red Mazda.

'Yes.' She smiled.

'I heard that red cars go faster—is that true?'

Kathryn laughed. 'Some might, but mine goes at the speed limit.'

'Very wise.' He nodded. 'I'll see you at the hospital, Kathryn. Thanks for an...interesting morning.'

'Yes—thanks, Jack. Perhaps we could have a re-match some time?'

'Good idea.' He grinned, his eyes gleaming with mischief. 'Let me get a little of my own back.'

'Ha,' she retorted, and unlocked her car. 'We'll see about that. Bye, Jack.' Kathryn was still grinning fifteen minutes later as she drove toward her apartment. She wound her way down South Road's steep hill to the Adelaide plains. Her smile disappeared as she stamped on the brakes, stopping too close for comfort to the car in front.

She slowly rounded another bend in the road and it became evident why the traffic was banked up—a five-car pile-up and, by the looks of things, it had only just happened. Kathryn inched into the left-hand lane, pulled her car off the road and flicked on her hazard lights. Reaching for the emergency medical kit she'd purchased only days ago, she jumped out of the car and ran toward the accident.

People were milling about everywhere, but after a quick assessment Kathryn realised the car in the centre of the crash had taken the brunt of the impacts.

'I'm a doctor,' she said loudly, and was bombarded by ten different voices at once. She calmed everyone down and assessed a few people who seemed to be more shaken than anything else.

'Please.' An elderly woman grabbed at her arm. 'My husband can't get out of the car. I managed to climb out the passenger window but the steering-wheel is crushed against my husband and he can't get out.'

'What's his name?' Kathryn asked as she followed the woman.

'Henry. This is our car.' She pointed to the car in the middle—two cars seemed glued to it on either end.

Kathryn poked her head through the passenger window. 'Hello, Henry. I'm Kathryn Pearce and I'm a doctor.' She looked at his face and noticed a cut on his forehead. There was also a bit of blood at the corner of his mouth. 'Where does it hurt the most?' she asked, and received no response. 'Henry.' She called his name again, this time louder than before. 'Henry, can you hear me?'

Kathryn noticed his eyes move and decided he'd probably bitten his tongue. His neck would be stiff and getting worse as whiplash set in. She turned and handed her medical kit to Henry's wife as she prepared to climb into the car. 'I'm presuming someone has called the police and ambulance?'

The wail of a siren in the distance answered her question. 'I need to assess him now. We can't wait for the ambulance.'

'Kathryn!' She turned as a familiar voice called her name. Jack. He was running down the hill towards the accident. Within seconds he'd reached her. His eyes quickly checked her. 'You're all right. Thank God. I thought you might have been injured.'

Kathryn gave him a quizzical look but now was not the time to reflect on his words. 'I'm going in to see Henry.' She motioned to the elderly man in the car. 'He's got a cut on his forehead and can't respond to my queries. The steering-wheel's crushed him in and he can't move.'

Jack assessed the situation. 'I'm too big to fit through the window. In you go.' He scooped her up without a word of warning and shoved her feet through the window. Men! Kathryn thought. They just had to take charge and be macho.

Turning her attention to Henry, she examined him quickly. His terrified eyes seemed to search hers and she reassured him. 'We're going to get you out. You'll be fine.' His pulse was thready and quite fast, indicating shock. She pulled her small torch from her kit and checked the contraction of his pupils. They were of equal size and retracting to light. Probably no brain damage but she couldn't be sure without X-rays.

Next, she shone the torch into his mouth and confirmed her earlier suspicions. Henry had bitten his tongue. She quickly ran her fingers along his neck and then gently over his arms and legs. She took his pulse again and noticed it was beginning to settle.

'He's just jammed,' she said to Jack, who'd poked his head through the window. 'He's bitten his tongue and I need some gauze to try and clean up the blood before I can get a good look at it. The cut on his forehead will need stitching but is OK for now.'

Kathryn held out her hand and Jack slapped a pair of gloves into her palm.

'Put them on first. Will you need to stitch the tongue here?'

'I haven't got the correct sutures in my kit. They'll have to cut the car open to get him out, Jack. He's well and truly stuck.'

They'd spoken in soft tones so as not to frighten their patient. Once Kathryn had the surgical gloves on, she reached for the gauze Jack held out to her. 'I'm just going to remove your dentures, Henry. It will make it easier for me to look at your tongue. I want to ask you a few questions and you can blink once for yes and twice for no. How's that sound?'

Henry blinked his eyes once for yes.

'Are you allergic to any drugs, such as pethidine?' Kathryn waited for his answer and when two blinks came she informed Jack. 'Is your neck stiff and sore?' She continued to wipe the blood from his mouth, tenderly examining the area. Her tactic was to keep Henry's mind occupied while she worked.

He answered her with one blink. 'Can you wiggle your toes?' She waited while Henry tried to wiggle his toes. One blink. 'Good.' She saw Henry's eyes flick over to Jack, who was drawing up the shot of pethidine. 'This is Jack. He's my boss,' she added in a stage whisper, 'so we'd better watch our p's and q's.'

For the first time Henry's eyes softened a little and Kathryn smiled. She was sure he was too stiff, and relaxing his muscles would do his body the world of good.

She administered the pethidine and within minutes Henry's eyelids closed. It wasn't a strong dose, but enough to take the top off his pain while the emergency crews cut him out.

'The ambulance and police are here,' Jack said, and left Kathryn alone with her patient. Now that Henry was dozing, Kathryn took a good look at his tongue. He'd almost bitten it half off. It needed the skilled hands of a plastic surgeon to fix it together again.

Kathryn looked out of the shattered windscreen as the paramedics assessed the injured people with Jack's expert help. Blue-uniformed police were writing furiously as they took statements. After what seemed an eternity, but which in reality was only a few minutes, she saw Jack lead the emergency teams in her direction.

From there everything happened at once. The 'jaws of life' were brought out and the top of Henry's car was peeled back like a can. He remained conscious but dozed as the steering-wheel was removed and the paramedics lifted him out.

'We'll be needing statements from you,' the sergeant said when Kathryn had been relieved of her patient.

'Certainly.' Jack answered for both of them. 'We're at the Children's hospital.' He reached into his wallet and pulled out his business card. 'My mobile number's on there so you can contact us when you're ready.' With that done, he placed an arm around Kathryn's waist and urged her in the direction of their cars.

'Where are we going?' she asked.

'Let's leave it to the experts and join the queue out of here. I've still got things to do—as have you,' he reminded her.

She accepted her medical kit back from him, realising he was right. They'd done all they could. It wasn't much when she thought about it but, she supposed, from Henry's point of view, having a doctor sitting beside him had eased his apprehensions.

'You were great.' Jack reassured her as though he could read her mind. 'Now, go and see your brother before he becomes worried about you.'

'Yes, boss,' she said, grinning at him.

The next time Kathryn saw Jack was at the weekly meeting on Tuesday. He was cool and aloof and said nothing of the morning they'd spent together. She wasn't sure what type of reaction she'd expected from him, Kathryn thought as she made her way to the ward.

Pushing Jack Holden and the confusing emotions he evoked to the back of her mind, she concentrated on doing a quick ward round before she tackled the mound of paperwork piled up on her desk.

Prudence Florington's operation had proceeded with no complications and, clinically speaking, she was well on the road to recovery. Mentally speaking, she was only happy when her sister was around.

'Good morning,' Kathryn said cheerfully as she entered the room. Penelope was sitting up in bed beside her sister while Sally read them a story. Kathryn reviewed Prudence's chart, taking note of the blood pressure and temperature readings.

She waited until Sally had finished the book, before proceeding with her examination. Prudence held onto her sister's hand but was very brave while Kathryn did what she had to.

'How's the pain been?' she asked Sally.

'Not too bad. She had a fretful night but was able to get some sleep when Gregory dropped Penelope off early this morning.'

'Good. Prudence,' Kathryn said quietly, 'do you hurt any-where?'

'Don't want 'Nelope to go,' she said, and clung to her sister. Kathryn's heart constricted and she briefly closed her eyes. She would have to do something about this. Prudence would recover more rapidly if Penelope was allowed to stay. She'd have to discuss it with Jack and reach some kind of compromise. At the moment Penelope was allowed to stay all day long, and it had been noted on Prudence's chart that she slept better when her twin was with her.

But the long nights were awash with broken sleep and crying fits. It was deep slumber that Prudence's little body needed to help mend her leg. Administering a sedative was an alternative, but one Kathryn wasn't willing to accept—not when the same thing could be accomplished by having her sister sleeping with her.

'Would you like Mummy to read you another story?' Sally asked and the little girls' attention was successfully diverted.

'I'll be around later this afternoon,' Kathryn said quietly to Sally, who simply nodded and began to read.

Kathryn made the necessary changes to Prudence's treatment chart and decided to take a quick trip to the cafeteria for some lunch, before settling down to her paperwork. She had just rounded the corner of the long corridor leading away from the wards when she saw Steven, all colour drained from his face, coming out of Professor Holden's office.

'What's the matter, Steven? You look awful,' she asked with sisterly concern.

'Thanks a lot,' he said, his words slightly slurred.

'You're drunk!' Kathryn was astonished. She reached for his arm and propelled him quickly to her own office. 'What on earth are you doing in the hospital grounds in *this* condition?'

'Not you too,' he groaned as he slumped down into a chair. 'I've just been put through the wringer by Professor Holden.'

'No wonder you looked so pale.' Kathryn sat down behind her desk and tried to keep calm. The look of remorse on her brother's face was enough punishment—for the moment. 'Tell me what happened.'

'I was just about to go home after an all-night stint in Theatre when I met up with some of the vascular registrars who were also finishing a night shift and going to the pub for breakfast. One of the guys is getting married this weekend so we started celebrating. I know.' He looked at her. 'It was wrong to start drinking when I was so tired and hadn't eaten much, but I did. I'm sorry, Kath.'

'So why were you in the hospital grounds?'

'I forgot my bag. I've got an exam in three days and I left my books here—in my bag—so I thought I'd make a quick detour, before going home. I never thought I'd get caught.'

'You know the hospital rules, Steven. Alcohol and intoxicated personnel are not permitted within hospital grounds. There were other options open to you, Steven. You could have called me and asked me to bring your books home.'

'I know. I just didn't think.' Steven ran a hand through his hair. 'I didn't think. That's the whole point here, isn't it?'

'I guess it is.' She was silent for a moment, then asked softly, 'What did Professor Holden have to say?'

'He said there will be a permanent record on my file regarding this incident and I'm to report to his office first thing tomorrow morning for disciplinary action.' He paused and hung his head. 'I'll more than likely fail my rotation because of this.' His words were muffled but Kathryn heard them.

'Perhaps I can have a word with him.'

'Big sister, fighting my battles for me. Now that would look really good on my record.'

'I don't intend to *fight* your battles, Steven, just lend a hand when I can. Now, why don't you go home before anyone else catches you and get some rest. We'll talk more later.'

'I'm really sorry, Kath. Your disappointment in me is enough retribution.' He stood and walked to the door. 'Oh, and, Kath.' He paused and gave her a crooked grin. 'Could you bring my books home?'

She shook her head and smiled. 'Yes. Now get going—and, Steven, take a taxi. To put my mind at ease,' she added when he was about to protest.

As soon as the door shut behind him Kathryn picked up the phone and dialled Jack's extension. When his secretary answered she asked to see him immediately, stating it was urgent.

'He's free at the moment, Dr Pearce.'

'Thank you. I'll be right there.'

A few minutes later she knocked on Jack's door, before hearing her summons to enter. He put his pen down when he saw her and leaned back in his chair.

'What can I do for you, Kathryn?'

Unsure what his reaction would be, she took a deep breath, before saying, 'I've come to discuss my brother with you.'

'Your brother?'

'Steven Pearce,' she supplied, and watched the look of dawning comprehension cross his face.

'I see,' he said slowly.

'I ran into him when he was leaving your office.'

'His behaviour has been inexcusable. I don't care whether he was on duty or not—his actions are unacceptable for an intern.'

'I agree. I've had a few words to say to him myself and will probably have a few more once he's sobered up.'

'Then why do you want to discuss it?'

'I'd like you to reconsider taking disciplinary action.'

'I don't think that's any of your business,' Jack replied, his temper rising. 'He is an intern attached to my rotation and I decide what action is to be taken. I do not get opinions from the rest of my staff. Relation or not, it's none of your business,' he reiterated.

'On that point, I disagree,' Kathryn said forcefully and clearly. Jack seemed unwilling to bend—even slightly—and she could feel her anger increasing by the second. 'Steven will make an excellent doctor and he doesn't need to have that kind of blemish on his record. He knows he's slipped up and will probably beat himself up emotionally for quite a while. Beside the fact that he's his own worst enemy, he values my opinion highly and is thoroughly ashamed at disappointing me.'

'You're very protective of your little brother, aren't you?'

'You've got siblings. Are you going to tell me that if the positions were reversed you wouldn't intervene on their behalf?' Kathryn took a few deep breaths and lowered her voice. Her next words were very important. 'He's sorry, Jack. *Really* sorry. He knows he messed up big time and, believe me, he won't do anything of the sort again.' She looked into his eyes and said imploringly, 'Please don't take official action. I know you're required to make a note of it on his file but don't take it any further than that.'

Feeling slightly drained, Kathryn sat down in the seat opposite his desk and waited.

'All right,' he said at last. 'There will be a permanent record on his file but I won't take any official action.'

'Thank you.' She smiled, her anger completely gone. 'I appreciate it, as will Steven.' Kathryn relaxed in her chair and looked at him. He was, without a doubt, a devastatingly handsome man, a man who evoked a different reaction within her every time she saw him.

'Was there anything else?' he asked softly, noticing her appraisal of him.

Quickly averting her eyes, she played with the end of her long braid while she tried to think up an excuse for her blatant stare.

'Kathryn,' he said quietly, and she looked up. He'd come around his desk and was sitting on the corner, half a metre away. He reached for her hands, which were still fidgeting with her hair, and pulled her up to stand before him.

Their eyes locked for a few moments before he cupped her face in his hands and brought his hungry mouth to hers. Kathryn groaned and knew she'd missed him more than she'd realised.

Fire seemed to lick through her body as his assault on her senses began. Jack's mouth was harsh and punishing on hers and she fleetingly wondered why. He gathered her close to his body and Kathryn knew she was a willing prisoner. She gave in to the passion and bit his bottom lip. He pulled back momentarily and glared. Slowly he raised his fingers to his lips and when he found no blood Kathryn gave a mirthless laugh.

'Should I bite harder next time?'

His only answer was to pull her between his legs and resume his onslaught. The fire that had previously raged through Kathryn's body was now fanned into a burning furnace. She plunged her fingers into the softness of his hair, urging him on as her breasts pressed against the cotton shirt that covered his manly chest.

Jack groaned and Kathryn gave herself up to the inevitable.

They'd been attracted to each other from the start. The playful kisses they'd exchanged at the archery park had only been a practice session for today.

His tongue delved deeper into her mouth, causing her to groan out loud. If she'd had any desire to hold back the extent of her attraction it had been blown away with a single touch from him. Kathryn matched his desire...his need...his wanting.

The telephone on his desk shrilled to life, startling Kathryn and breaking the contact.

'Ignore it,' he ordered, unwilling to release her.

'But your secretary knows you're in here.' Kathryn tried to reason as she slowly pulled away.

Keeping one arm firmly around her waist, Jack snaked out a hand to silence the intrusive noise.

'Yes,' he snapped, and Kathryn tried to squirm out of his hold. 'I'm busy. Call me in half an hour.' Without waiting for a reply, he slammed the phone down.

'Who...who was it?' Kathryn asked in an attempt to divert him. She was beginning to feel uncomfortable.

'No one of consequence.' He replaced his other arm around her and pulled her toward him. 'Now.' His voice was husky with desire. 'Where were we?'

'Jack...please,' she implored.

'Please what?' He raised his eyebrows and gave her a fiendish grin, but when she refused to play his game, he let her go.

'I think I should be going.' As if to support her statement, her stomach grumbled. 'I was on my way to the cafeteria when I ran into Steven. I'd better go and get some food.' She knew she was babbling as she backed to the door, but couldn't help it. 'Thanks again for not taking any disciplinary action with Steven. I'll have a word with him when I get home and talk some sense into him.'

'You live together?'

'Why not? I lived with him while we were growing up. Why should now be any different?'

'Doesn't having a little brother around...cramp your style?'

'No,' she frowned. 'We're both adults.'

'Good. Then he won't be embarrassed when I pick you up

on Saturday morning. I've already checked the rosters and I know you're not on emergency call.'

'Why would you be picking me up?' she asked a little hesitantly as her back came into contact with the door. She reached behind her and turned the knob, waiting for his answer.

'So we can have a rematch. You did cheat on the last target, if I recall correctly. Surely I deserve an opportunity to rectify the situation.'

Kathryn nodded. All she needed to do at the moment was to get as far away from Jack Holden as possible. The man was dangerous with a capital D. He made her lose herself completely and if she needed anything around him, it was self-control.

'O.K. What time?'

'I'll pick you up at eight a.m.'

'Fine.' She opened the door and was halfway out before he called her name.

'Be ready, Kathryn. I don't like to be kept waiting.'

She couldn't think of anything to say to his high and mighty attitude so she pulled a face at him before closing the door.

CHAPTER FOUR

IN THE cafeteria, Kathryn bought a salad roll and, after collecting a cup of coffee, sat down at a table by herself. Her mind raced over the past few minutes she'd spent alone with Jack. He'd caused her to experience a complete range of emotions, but there was one thing of which Kathryn was certain. She liked him. Which, she thought, was just as well, considering the animal magnetism they felt toward each other.

'Mind if I sit down?' Joan asked.

'Sure. I could use some company.' As well as taking my mind off Professor Holden, she added silently.

'You seem to have settled in well,' Joan said as she began to eat her lunch. 'How's little Prudence coming along?'

'Oh, darn,' Kathryn said raising her hand to her forehead. 'I forgot to ask Jack about her. I want Penelope to stay with her sister full-time. Prudence is only going to make a complete recovery if her twin sister is with her twenty-four hours a day. It also means that at least one parent, if not both, will need to stay as well.'

'She needs her sister. You're Head of Orthopaedics—why don't you simply make the decision? I presume you've discussed this with Clara?'

'Yes. Clara's a great social worker. She's spoken to both parents, observed the girls and agrees with me. I simply wanted to get Jack's all-clear before I did anything. If I'd been here longer I probably wouldn't have hesitated but considering...' She let the sentence hang and sighed. 'Guess I'd better eat up and get back to the professor's office.'

'He's a great guy, isn't he?' Joan asked. 'I've really enjoyed working for him over the past few years. He's reasonable, easy to talk to and I've no doubt at all he'll agree to your treatment plan for Prudence. He always says that the kids come first and that's the way it should be.'

Kathryn nodded and kept on eating. She'd hoped to steer the conversation away from Jack, but Joan was in full swing of her high praise for him. 'And he's so handsome, too. If I were twenty years younger I'd be after him—make no mistake. Well,' she amended, 'twenty years younger and single. I'd have to be single or my darling Ian would have a fit.' She chuckled.

Curious to know a little bit more about Jack's love life, Kathryn probed. 'Does he have a steady girlfriend?'

'Not him. In the two years I've known him he's been seen with a different social beauty nearly every month. Sometimes two in a month. They don't last longer than four weeks.' Joan looked around to see if anyone was listening, before leaning closer to Kathryn.

'The hospital grapevine says he was in love with a woman but she died some years ago. Apparently, he blames himself for her death and therefore doesn't want to have any emotional attachments. He was too hurt and remembering is too painful.'

'Really?' Kathryn asked. 'Does anyone know who she was? What happened? Why does he blame himself?'

'No. It's only rumour. Probably none of it's true. He's just a normal, healthy male with an appetite for pretty young women. Who can blame him?'

'Who, indeed?' Kathryn agreed as she digested not only her late lunch but this information as well. She swallowed the last of her coffee and stood. 'I'd better have a word with Jack and then do another ward round. I promised Sally Florington I'd see her this afternoon.'

'A doctor's work is never done,' Joan quipped.

'The same could be said for the nursing staff,' Kathryn replied with a smile, and walked off—back to the panther's lair.

Jack wasn't in his office but his secretary was able to call him for her to speak to. She discussed the case with him and received the go-ahead. Next, she informed the nursing staff of the changes and asked for the best way to accommodate the whole family. Everyone agreed that the twins should be kept together and were willing to help out. An extra folding bed and portable cot were squeezed into the small private room.

'The family that plays together stays together,' Sally joked.

'I know Prudence would rather have Penelope in her bed, but the traction can't be disturbed. We'll push the cot beside the bed and they can at least hold hands through the safety rails.'

'Thank you, Kathryn. Gregory and I appreciate all you've done. It means a lot to us both.'

'It's not only me,' she replied, unwilling to take the credit for an obvious solution. 'The whole ward agreed it was the best thing to do. In the morning we can fold the beds up and wheel the cot out, which will give you more room to sit and play with the girls.'

'Prudence will be so happy. It's been breaking my heart, having to separate them in the evenings. This solution means Gregory and I can spend time together once the girls are asleep.'

'Just let the nursing staff know to keep an eye on them and you can go down to the cafeteria for a romantic dinner for two. Of course, you'll have everyone else in the hospital there so it won't be secluded.'

Sally laughed. 'No different to sitting in a five-star restaurant,' she pointed out.

'In fact,' Kathryn said, 'I'll arrange it for tonight—my treat.'

Sally hugged her. 'Thanks, Kathryn. That would be wonderful.'

It didn't take long for Kathryn to make the necessary arrangements and the nursing staff were willing to help in any way they could. Finally, Kathryn walked to the car park, a mountain of paperwork in her briefcase which she'd decided would have more chance of getting done once she'd arrived home, eaten dinner and had a relaxing bath. Oh, the life of a doctor—and she loved it.

The next time Kathryn saw Jack was late on Thursday afternoon. She had just finished her operating list and was sitting in the doctors' lounge, writing up case notes on her last patient.

'How are you feeling?' he asked.

'Why do you ask?' She didn't look up and made a few more notes, before signing her name. Closing the folder, she looked up at him. 'What's the problem?'

'Feel like going back to Theatre?' He rested his hands on her shoulders and began to gently massage her taut trapezius muscle.

Kathryn sighed and closed her eyes. 'What's happened?'

'School bus crash out at a conservation park down south near Victor Harbour.'

She was having difficulty concentrating on his words as his fingers worked their magic. 'I think you'd better stop that or I'll be asleep in no time,' she warned.

'Can't have that,' he joked, but stopped all the same. 'Especially when I'm about to send you back to Theatre for a few more hours. Why don't we go down to Casualty for an update on the situation?'

'Sure.' She stood and stretched her arms above her head. 'Guess there's no point in changing.' Kathryn glanced down at her theatre clothes and shrugged. 'Lead on.'

On the way to Casualty, Jack told her what he knew. 'End of a day excursion, with thirty girls on a chartered bus. The weather's been quite miserable down there for most of the day and, as you know, most conservation parks have gravel roads.

'The driver was negotiating the potholes when a kangaroo jumped in front of the bus. He swerved and hit some loose gravel, shot across the road, through the bushes, rolled a couple of times and finally came to rest in a gully.

'The bus was upside down when the ride ended and most of the children sustained minor injuries. One of the girls was sent to find help and came across some campers who notified the park ranger and raised the alarm.'

'What about the driver?' Kathryn asked as they walked into Casualty.

'He's been flown by helicopter to Adelaide General Hospital where he'll probably be undergoing surgery. There were three girls bad enough to be sent to us—the rest have been taken to Victor Harbour hospital. The retrieval team should be landing soon with our patients.'

They found the casualty sister just replacing the phone. She looked up at them with relief. 'I was just about to have you both paged.'

'Do you have more details for us?'

'Yes. Of the three girls who are due here soon, one of them, a Chantal McBain, seems to be the most serious. She was apparently standing in the aisle when the incident took place. When the bus began to roll she was thrown through a window. She has multiple fractures as well as concussion.'

'Contact Radiology and have them waiting for her,' Jack said.

'Do we have a list of her fractures?' Kathryn asked.

'Yes. Her right shoulder is dislocated but the retrieval team didn't want to manipulate it, without having X-rays to check that neither scapula nor top of the humerus were fractured. She has a Colles' fracture to her right wrist, fractured phalanges on her left foot and a busted-up left knee. From what the retrieval team reported, the patella is very bad.'

'When can we expect them?' Jack asked.

'In another fifteen minutes.'

'What about the other two children?' Kathryn was mentally going over her available staff.

'Both have fractured arms, which will probably need surgery to fix and stabilise the bones. Needless to say, all are battered and bruised,' the sister added. 'I've got three treatment rooms set up and have called in extra nursing staff. Emergency Theatres have been notified and are getting things ready.'

'Page Dr Harris and have him organise treatment and Theatre for the two broken arms. I'll also need him in Theatre with me if we have some major surgery to perform on this girl's knee. What did you say her name was again?'

'Chantal McBain. Aged thirteen.'

'Family?'

'All have been notified and are on their way in.'

'Standard protocol, Sister,' Jack said. 'The last thing we need is any extra emotional disturbances when the families get here.'

'Yes, Professor. Now, if you'll both excuse me, I'll get these things organised.'

Jack turned to Kathryn. 'Let's have a quick coffee before we begin.' He led her to the small doctors' tearoom just to the left of the emergency theatres. 'It sounds as though it's mainly orthopaedic injuries but I'd like all three, especially Chantal, to have head X-rays.'

'Agreed.'

'If it shows just a minor concussion there should be no problem with anaesthetics. Who's on call tonight for anaesthetics?'

'Frances Gray. In fact, I saw her up in Theatres just before I did my last case so hopefully she's still about and can organise some staff for us.'

'I'll have her paged immediately,' Jack said, and crossed to the wall phone. He also contacted Radiology and fired off a list of instructions. Checking his watch, he said, 'Time to go, Kathryn. Let's see what awaits us.'

The retrieval team had been one hundred per cent correct. One glance at Chantal McBain's knee and Kathryn knew it would need extensive reconstructive surgery.

'Hi, Chantal,' Kathryn said softly. 'I'm Dr Kathryn Pearce.' She looked down into scared blue eyes and tenderly brushed a few strands of blonde hair away from her face. 'I'll be taking you to Theatre very soon but first you need to have some X-rays taken.'

Chantal closed her eyes and a small tear squeezed its way out. Her face was tear-stained and grubby. Her clothes were torn, probably so that the retrieval team could tend and stabilise her wounds.

'You're going to be fine. We're here to help you,' Kathryn said reassuringly. The eyes remained closed and her patient's face relaxed as she slipped into unconsciousness. 'Get that head X-rayed immediately,' she said to the nurse. 'I believe Jack's in Radiology, waiting for her.'

The other two patients weren't nearly as bad, and after an initial assessment she left them in her registrar's capable hands.

'The other two girls,' Dr Harris informed her once initial X-rays had been taken, 'will require open reduction and internal fixation of their respective arms. I've organised for Noel Kaplo to do one and I'll do the other. It should, therefore, be about forty to fifty minutes until I can join you with the knee reconstruction.'

'Fine. In the meantime, I can attend to Chantal's other injuries.' She turned to Jack who'd just walked into the treatment room where they were viewing the radiographs. 'How does Chantal's skull look, Jack?'

'No fractures but, from reported symptoms, definitely a minor concussion. She will have painful headaches for the next few weeks but, apart from that, there'll be no other problems.'

'Are her parents here yet?' she asked Dr Harris.

'I'm not sure. I'll check with Sister. Do you want to speak with them?'

'Yes. I'd like to explain the procedures and get the permission forms signed.'

'I'll organise it for you,' Dr Harris said, and left Jack and Kathryn alone.

'Looks like you've been let off the hook,' Kathryn said.

'Yes. Nevertheless, I think I'll stick around.'

'As you wish,' she replied, her attention focused on the X-ray of Chantal's knee. 'I'd really prefer to have some three-dimensional scans done on this knee before I attempt to reconstruct it. Look.' She pointed to the screen. 'She's torn all the ligaments and muscles. The anterior cruciate ligament and posterior cruciate ligament will take at least six to eight months of rehabilitation until they're back in working order. This poor girl has a rough time ahead of her.'

Dr Harris knocked on the open door. 'I've put Mr and Mrs McBain into the family waiting room for you, Dr Pearce.'

'Thank you. Dr Harris,' she called as he started to retreat, 'could you organise a set of 3D scans on Chantal's knee? I'd like them before I start the reconstruction.'

'Right away.'

Alone again, Jack gave Kathryn a beaming smile. 'Go to work, Dr Pearce, and don't forget our date on Saturday morning.'

'How could I? You remind me of it at every turn.'

'I just want a chance to even things up.'

'You'll get your chance,' she said, and returned his smile. 'Now, if you'll excuse me, I have to go and explain this operation to some worried parents.'

Kathryn unhooked the X-rays and took them with her into

the family waiting room. The resemblance between Chantal and her mother was evident.

'Mr and Mrs McBain, I'm Dr Kathryn Pearce and I'll be the consultant in charge of your daughter's care.'

'Is she going to be all right?' Mrs McBain asked. She was a slender woman in her late thirties and had the same long blonde hair and blue eyes as her daughter. Mr McBain was well over six feet but had short, jet black hair and green eyes. They made a handsome couple, whose every thought was focused on their daughter.

'In the long term—yes. What I'd like to do now is go over her injuries with you and explain the procedures I'll be performing.' She waited for their nod of consent.

'Firstly, let me say, Chantal has been reviewed by our professor of neurosurgery and he's diagnosed only a minor concussion. This is good news. It means she'll only suffer minor headaches in the next few weeks. As for her orthopaedic injuries, her right shoulder is dislocated and we'll put it back in once she's anaesthetised.'

'I thought dislocations could be put back without any trouble?' Mr McBain queried.

'Sometimes they can. Generally with an accident such as Chantal's, we prefer to check that neither the shoulder nor the top of the arm have been fractured first. An X-ray has confirmed there are no breaks, and although I could quite easily put it back in now it's also a very painful procedure. Once she's anaesthetised it won't cause her any extra stress in terms of pain.

'She's broken her right wrist—what we call a Colles' fracture. This is a common injury when people fall onto their outstretched hands, which is what we presume happened to Chantal. I need to fix the fracture together and put a plaster cast on her wrist, which should stay on for approximately six to eight weeks.'

Mrs McBain gave a watery smile. 'She'll be able to get all of her friends to sign it.'

Kathryn smiled also. 'Yes, she will. Her other fractures include the two little toes on her left foot, which, according to the X-ray...' Kathryn pulled out the X-ray and held it up to the ceiling light, pointing to the toes in question '...will heal quite nicely by themselves. We can't put plaster around the toes so instead they'll be firmly strapped for six to eight weeks.' Kathryn lowered the radiograph and looked at the McBains.

'Chantal's main injury is to her knee. I would say it took the majority of her weight when she fell and the doctors who attended her at the accident site said they found traces of her blood on a nearby rock. This leads us to conclude that she's smashed the kneecap against this rock, which has caused the damage.'

'Will she walk again?' Mrs McBain raised a handkerchief to dab at her eyes.

'Yes,' Kathryn said firmly. 'In approximately six to eight months the ligaments of the knee should be fully restored but the physiotherapist will have her up and about in no time. Youth is wonderful at healing.'

'Oh, thank you, Dr Pearce. You don't know what it means to us when you say that.' Mrs McBain reached out for her husband's hand, a tearful smile on her face.

'Please, call me Kathryn. Chantal's been a very lucky girl. This next year won't be at all easy for her but she'll get through it just fine with your support.'

'So, what exactly has happened to her knee?' Mr McBain asked.

Kathryn pulled out another X-ray of Chantal's knee and held it up to the light. 'As you can see here, the kneecap, or patella, is badly dislocated. These X-rays, unfortunately, don't show the muscles, ligaments or cartilage but when the knee dislocated it pulled everything else out of place.'

'I had a cartilage removed a few years ago,' Mr McBain said, and Kathryn nodded.

'Good. Then you'll at least understand some of the pain and frustration Chantal will experience in the next few weeks. She's damaged both the front and back ligaments that stabilise the knee joint.

'The meniscus, which is probably what you injured, Mr McBain, absorbs weight within the knee and provides more stability. It's commonly known as cartilage and there are two around the knee.

'Chantal's cartilage is also torn so we'll be tidying it up. Her ligaments, as I said, will need extensive physiotherapy and re-habilitation over the next six to eight months, as will her muscles and tendons. The good news is that the damage is repairable.'

Dr Harris knocked on the door. 'Excuse me, Dr Pearce. We're ready for you.'

'Thank you. Dr Harris, could you go through the permission forms with Mr and Mrs McBain and answer any questions they might have?' She turned back to the parents. 'I'll let you know the results of the surgery as soon as I can.'

'How long will that be?' Mr McBain asked.

'Not for at least another three to four hours. It all depends on exactly what I find. Feel free to go home and freshen up or go and have a meal. Once Chantal comes around from the anaesthetic you'll want to be with her. She'll be needing you both to be refreshed and happy. If you do decide to leave the hospital, give Dr Harris your contact numbers and we can call you when we're finished.'

Mr McBain stood up and held out his hand. 'Thank you, Kathryn.'

'You're welcome.' She smiled, before leaving them with Dr Harris.

Kathryn reviewed the three-dimensional reconstructive X-rays which showed her exactly where all the pieces of bone were. She pushed them back into the packet and walked into the theatre prep room.

'Kathryn,' Theatre Sister said, 'Frances is just about to an-aesthetise so let's get you scrubbed.' She reached out a hand for the X-ray packet. 'I'll take those and get them up on the viewing box.'

Kathryn scrubbed and surveyed the knee. The ligaments and cartilage were the main problem. The arteries and veins were all stabilised and Kathryn was thankful to the wonderful pro-fessionals who worked on the retrieval teams.

Chantal's shoulder was relocated without complication and her wrist fracture was reduced and fixed with a plaster of Paris cast. Her swollen toes were reviewed and then restrapped.

An hour into Theatre, Kathryn checked the clock again, hop-ing Dr Harris would walk in at any minute. She scanned the X-rays of the patella and went over the procedure in her mind. Knee reconstruction was not something she did every day. Many adults, especially athletes, incurred the procedure, but not a thirteen-year-old girl.

'There you are, Dr Harris,' Theatre Sister said when he entered the room. Kathryn turned to face him.

'How are the other two patients?' she enquired from behind her mask.

'Both conditions stable. No complications with the surgery. I've just come from Recovery where they're in capable hands.'

'Excellent,' Kathryn replied. Dr Harris was a very good registrar. 'Let's see if we can get Chantal into the same capable hands as soon as possible.'

The knee reconstruction took another hour and a half but finally, after several check X-rays, Kathryn was satisfied with the outcome. 'The rest is up to you, my dear,' she said to the sleeping Chantal. The child looked so much younger than thirteen and Kathryn knew the road ahead was going to be rough for her. She only hoped that Chantal and her family could get through this tragedy. For not only did she have physical wounds to heal but mental and emotional ones as well, assuming she recalled being thrown from the out-of-control bus.

Wearily, Kathryn de-gowned, pulled off her theatre cap and mask and threw them into the bin, before making her way to the family waiting room. There was no sign of Chantal's parents and she quickly placed a call to Casualty Sister to notify the McBains that surgery had gone well and Chantal would be in Recovery in another half-hour.

At last she slumped into a chair in the doctors' tearoom and put her feet up on the table. She stretched and gave a big yawn, smothering it with her hand just as she heard the door open behind her.

'Finished at last, eh?' Jack's deep voice sent a tingle down her spine. She dredged up a smile for him as he sat opposite her. He reached for Kathryn's feet and lifted them off the table. Then he took off her shoes and placed her stockinged feet in his lap. Tenderly, he began to massage her left foot and Kathryn closed her eyes, feeling her tension begin to disappear.

Neither of them spoke while Jack continued with his prescription for relaxing. When Kathryn's head began to nod toward her chest Jack slowly stood up, placing her feet on the chair he vacated. He knelt beside her.

'Kathryn.' His voice was a whisper.

'Mmm,' she replied, turning her head to rest against his.

'Come on. It's time for you to go home. I'd be quite happy to drive you.'

As though waking from a dream, Kathryn opened her eyes and looked directly into Jack's. 'What did you say?' she asked as comprehension began to dawn on her.

'I said I'd take you home. You're bushed and you need to get to bed.'

'Yes, I do,' she said, and stretched again. Her arms extended over her head, she belatedly realised what a provocative gesture it was and quickly lowered her arms.

Jack chuckled. 'Awake now?'

'Getting there.' She bent and put her shoes on, then stood. 'Thanks for unknotting my feet. I'm sure when I finally arrive home I'll be asleep before my head hits the pillow.'

'Just make sure it's once you get home. I don't want you falling asleep behind the wheel. Why don't I follow you to make sure you get home safely?'

'Don't be ridiculous,' she told him. 'I'll be perfectly all right. I'm wide awake now. Besides, I have to get changed and check on Chantal and the other two girls before I can even begin to think about leaving. No, you go on home, Jack. I'm sure you've been on your feet just as much as I have today, and both of us have clinics and meetings and all sorts of things tomorrow morning and—'

'Kathryn,' he interrupted her. 'Shh.' He gathered her close and pressed her head against his shoulder. 'It was just an offer. A simple yes or no would have been sufficient.'

Kathryn closed her eyes and sighed. They stood still for a few moments before she pulled back and looked up into his hypnotic blue eyes.

'But I will give you one thing,' he murmured, his mouth dangerously close to hers.

'What's that?' she whispered.

'This.' He lowered his head a fraction more until their lips met. It had been a whole two days since he'd kissed her and she realised she'd been impatiently waiting for it to happen again. Gently he pulled away. 'Change, check on your patients, then home and bed. I probably won't be seeing you tomorrow as I have a hectic schedule. Saturday. Don't forget.'

She smiled at his words. 'I won't. See you at eight a.m. Sharp.'

The following day Kathryn was extremely pleased with Chantal's progress and requested that she be moved from Intensive Care to the ward.

'I just want to wash my hair,' Chantal pleaded after Kathryn had given her a thorough examination. 'I can't believe how badly my face is scratched and bruised. How am I ever going to enter for that teen-girl beauty contest now?' The last question, thankfully, was directed to her mother. Mrs McBain soothed her daughter as best she could.

'We have a hairdresser assigned to the hospital,' said Kathryn. 'I'll make sure she's contacted to come around and get you fixed up.'

'Thank you,' Mrs McBain said.

'I won't be around to see you tomorrow but Dr Harris will be able to answer any questions you might have regarding your treatment.' Kathryn pasted a smile onto her face and made a quick exit to the sister's desk where she updated Chantal's case notes.

Roll on tomorrow, Kathryn thought as she went back to her office to catch up on her paperwork.

On Saturday morning, at precisely seven fifty-five a.m., Kathryn was standing under the shelter outside her front door, waiting for Jack to arrive. The light rain didn't bother her—in fact, she decided, it added to the freshness of the morning.

She was dressed comfortably in denim jeans with a colourful woollen jumper on top. Underneath she wore a russet-red long-sleeved bodysuit that hugged all her curves. She'd pulled her hair back into a low ponytail instead of the braid she had for work.

Her shoes were practical leather walking shoes. She wasn't going to a fashion parade, she reminded herself, but an archery park. If Jack didn't like the casual way she dressed, that was his problem.

Four and a half minutes later Jack's black Jaguar convertible came round the corner. He'd put the soft top up, ensuring the leather seats didn't get wet. Kathryn had seen the car a few times and was sure her appreciation showed.

'Like Jaguars?' he asked, coming around the car to hold the door for her. He, too, was dressed in jeans, although his were black denim and he wore a black, tight-fitting, fine wool turtle-neck which Kathryn knew would drive her crazy.

'Yes,' she replied, and tore her eyes from his body. 'What type is it?'

'XK 120. I always loved them as a child and promised myself that when I could afford it I'd buy one. She wasn't in very good condition when I bought her so I had her restored.'

'Why do all men refer to their cars as *she*? It's always puzzled me,' Kathryn said as she buckled her seat belt. Jack put the car in motion.

'Perhaps it's because a man's car is the only female who won't talk back, doesn't need pampering, doesn't nag, isn't emotionally dependent, never gets angry if you don't pick up your dirty underwear—'

'All right. All right. I'm sorry I asked. It's obviously a guy thing that women will never understand so I'm sorry I opened such a big can of worms.'

'Ah-h, worms. Now there's a subject I'm sure I can interest you in. Especially considering today's weather.' He gave her a quick sideways glance. 'The rain doesn't bother you?'

'No. I quite like it.' She smiled at him as realisation dawned. 'Did you expect me to ring and cancel just because of few drops from above?'

'Well, yes. Quite frankly, I did.'

'I have news for you, Professor Holden. I'm not like all those other bimbos you date whose hair, make-up or nails can be ruined by a little precipitation.'

'You forgot the new dress.'

'What?'

'Their dresses get ruined as well. Obviously that has never happened to you.'

'It has, as a matter of fact, but material possessions don't mean as much to me as some other women.'

Jack gave a hearty chuckle. 'Good for you.'

Surprisingly enough, there was no lack of running conversation to the archery park. After they'd signed in, gone to their separate lockers and collected their equipment, they were ready to begin.

'I like the fact the membership price includes a locker to store your equipment in. At my club in Melbourne,' Kathryn said as they walked out to the first target, 'I had to take my stuff home with me and bring it back each time. This is much more convenient.'

When they reached the target Jack turned to her and said seriously, 'How about a few ground rules?'

'I knew that was coming. Don't you trust me?'

'Definitely not, just as you don't trust me either. First of all, if you hit a bullseye with any deliberate distraction or disturbance you get an extra fifty points.'

'I like the sound of that.' Kathryn grinned. She'd expected him to be serious but, apparently, Jack was out for as much fun as he could get. She'd better be on her guard. If his antics from last time were any indication, she'd be throwing herself at him in the bushes and begging him to make love to her. The thought made her go hot and cold as she tried to concentrate on his words.

'Any lost arrows bring a point score of twenty for the person who finds it, and at the end of the game the loser has to buy dinner at the winner's choice of restaurant.'

'When?'

'Tonight,' he said, his eyes gleaming with excitement. 'I love Japanese food. Do you?'

'Yes, but that's irrelevant because I prefer Italian and I'll be winning, my dear professor.'

'Let's seal the deal with a kiss and we can begin.'

'Let's seal it with a handshake,' she amended, and he shrugged. Jack put out his hand, but the moment Kathryn put hers into it he pulled her close and kissed her briefly on the lips.

'Rat!' she said when he let her go.

'You're going to have to think up better names to call me than that, Kathryn.'

'Don't worry,' she replied as he got ready to shoot. 'I've been reading the big book of name-calling. I borrowed it from your secretary.' She watched as he drew his elbow back and concentrated on the target. Bullseye. Kathryn tried to think of a way to distract him but was too distracted herself by his gorgeous body. She was positive he'd worn such tight fitting clothes exactly for this purpose—to put her off guard.

A few targets later, as Kathryn was fitting her arrow into the string, she wondered whether Jack was trying to psych her out. He hadn't performed one stunt and she was beginning to turn into a nervous wreck.

She took her aim and focused on that centre ring.

'Magpie!' Jack called. 'It's swooping!'

A smile touched Kathryn's face, but apart from that she didn't move. 'Wrong season,' she told him blandly, and let the arrow go. 'It's the end of winter, Jack,' she said as she turned to face him. 'Magpies don't start swooping until spring. I got the bullseye so does that mean I score extra points?'

Her heart turned over as he ran his thumb and forefinger along his chin. He was a handsome man. The problem was that he knew it. 'That *was* an attempt at distraction, wasn't it?' she queried, just to make sure.

'It was. You get the extra points. I was just thinking, I'll have to resort to more drastic measures.' He raised his eyebrows and grinned, before walking off in the direction of the next target.

The light rain had stopped and a bit of sun peeped through the clouds. Although walking through the bush from target to target wasn't all that strenuous, Kathryn was beginning to feel a little warm with her jumper on.

She was about to stop and take it off when an idea dawned. She waited until Jack was ready to take his shot and, positive she was standing in his peripheral vision, slowly and seductively eased her jumper up and over her head.

It worked. His concentration broke and he accidentally let go of the string. The arrow sailed through the air, passed the target and disappeared into the bush. He didn't throw a tantrum or run off after his arrow. He simply stood where he was and watched the show.

Jack wolf-whistled and Kathryn grinned as she tied the jumper around her waist. It was the only practical place for it to go. Feeling brazen, she wiggled her hips and said in her best Sophia Loren voice, 'You like?'

'Yes, I do,' he said. 'You are a very attractive woman, Kathryn Pearce.' Within a few short strides he'd closed the distance between them.

'The arrow,' Kathryn said, all attempt at seduction dropped. 'We should find your arrow.' Jack placed his bow on the ground and clamped his arms about her waist. 'Twenty extra points, remember?'

'But there's another rule that needs to be taken care of first.'

'Wh-what's that?' She gazed up into his eyes which were pools of desire.

'A victory kiss for successfully disturbing me. Did I forget to mention that rule?'

'You know you did.' She placed her hands on his chest but couldn't push him away. 'I didn't agree to that rule so it doesn't count.'

'Oh, yes, it does, honey,' he said as he lowered his head. When his lips met hers Kathryn sighed with pleasure. Each time he kissed her she became more and more addicted. His mouth moved over hers a few more times before he pulled away.

'It's arrow-finding time. Twenty points up for grabs.' He walked off in the direction the arrow was last seen and began to scour the ground with his eyes. Kathryn breathed in deeply and slowly exhaled. Jack Holden was more than she could handle.

A few targets later they were doing the same thing—hunting

for an arrow. Except this time it was Kathryn's. Jack had successfully distracted her by running the tip of the arrow up the inside of her leg. Goosebumps had instantly covered her body and her heartbeat had doubled.

She didn't let him kiss her this time, knowing if she did they'd end up in the bushes and the game would be forgotten. Instead, she stalked off into the bush only to hear him chuckle softly behind her. Thankfully, he didn't say a thing.

'We'll never find it,' Kathryn said after nearly fifteen minutes of looking. 'I don't even know which direction it went.'

'Sensitive on the inside of your leg, are you?' He chuckled again. 'I'll have to remember that.'

'I give up. We've only got one more target to go and you've won anyway so it doesn't really matter.'

'If you insist,' he said, and led the way to the final target.

Kathryn had been so put off by his physique, his kisses, his overall masculine presence that her shooting had been extremely off. But at least, she thought as she followed him up the dirt path, I've successfully managed to bring his score down by quite a hefty chunk. She was sure Jack wasn't shooting as well as he usually did either. The bodysuit she was wearing certainly deserved quite a bit of the credit for that.

On his last arrow Kathryn decided to give it one more try. After all, she had nothing to lose.

'Cute butt,' she called out as he stood with his feet apart and put his arrow onto the string. Kathryn crept up behind him, and when he was about to let go she pinched his behind.

Jack jumped a metre into the air and spun to face her. Amazingly enough, his arrow had pierced the bullseye and he'd won the match by at least three hundred points.

Kathryn began to back away as he advanced. 'Good one, Kathryn. Now, do you want your kiss?'

She shook her head. 'I don't deserve it.'

'Oh, yes, you do,' he said. He seemed to love this stalking game.

'No, I mean the arrow. It's in the bullseye. Look!' She pointed over his shoulder. He stopped and turned, amazed, to see she was telling the truth.

'Well I'll be...' he said, letting his words trail off. 'Not bad, eh?' She could see the success going to his head. He turned back to face her. 'I still think you should get your kiss.'

'No.' Kathryn held up her hand. 'Enough kisses for this morning. Why don't we save some for tonight when I have to eat crow and take you out to dinner?' All she needed at the moment was a break from his natural boyish charms. Charms that were causing havoc with her senses. She needed a few hours to regroup and arm herself for the next onslaught.

'That's right,' he said, and he stopped advancing. 'But you won't be eating crow, Kathryn. Perhaps raw fish. I said Japanese and I know the perfect place. Now, why don't we go and have an early lunch and sort out the details?'

'Sounds good.' Kathryn breathed a sigh of relief. It was much safer to be in the club house. Whoever had said there was safety in numbers had obviously met Jack Holden.

That evening Kathryn put gold hoop earrings through her pierced ears and stood back to study her reflection. She ran her hands over her hips as the black crêpe fabric clung to her body like a second skin.

The dress was long and if it hadn't been for the two-inch black heels she wore, the material would have swept the floor. There was a split in the back of the dress and when she walked it revealed a good length of thigh.

She'd decided on impulse to leave her hair loose, tucking it behind her ears. Kathryn had never been one to wear a lot of make-up and so applied only a light covering. Effective use of mascara and earthy-toned eyeshadow emphasised her eyes. A quick brush of blusher gave colour to her face, and she finished it off with a touch of lipstick.

She puckered up and blew a kiss to her reflection, before reaching for her silk shawl. It had taken her a while to decide on this dress as its halter-neck top would leave her feeling cold. But, she'd reasoned, she'd be sitting in a warm car and then a warm restaurant so it didn't really matter.

Japanese. Kathryn liked the food but was hopeless with the eating implements. She sincerely hoped the restaurant would have a fork or spoon, instead of making her use chopsticks. Her family had laughed at her lack of co-ordination over the years. She could perform a total hip replacement operation but couldn't use chopsticks.

The doorbell rang and Kathryn's heart leapt into her throat. Her body tingled in anticipation at seeing Jack again. Which was ridiculous, she told herself as she collected her handbag and went to the door, considering it was only five and a half hours since he'd dropped her back home after their long and very pleasant lunch.

'Hi,' Jack drawled. For a moment their eyes travelled the length of each other's body before they met again. Jack was dressed to kill in black dress trousers, chambray shirt and silk tie—he momentarily took her breath away.

Kathryn swallowed and smiled, unsure of what to say or do.

'Ready?' he asked.

'Yes,' she replied, giving her head a little shake in order to clear the fuzziness from it.

Jack placed his hand under her elbow as she walked down the wet path towards the Jaguar. He held her door open and seated her inside, before going around to the driver's side.

The easy camaraderie they'd shared earlier that morning had disappeared. Kathryn marvelled that a change of clothes could make conversation so different. Or, perhaps, she reflected, after their fun-filled morning they were more aware of each other.

'You look...breathtaking. I like it when you wear your hair down.'

Kathryn shrugged but was secretly happy with his compliment. 'It's more practical to braid it for work and tie it back at other times. I've been thinking of cutting it.'

'Don't.' The word was out of his mouth before Kathryn had finished speaking. 'Please don't cut it. It suits you.'

She gave him a sidelong glance. What was that about? Why should he care what she did with her hair? 'It was just a thought,' she replied, and asked about the restaurant in a bid to change the subject.

'It's not too far away, just up in the Adelaide hills. I came across it quite by accident and since then, I've eaten there quite regularly.'

'Ah,' Kathryn said with a smile, and he gave her a brief look. 'So this is where you bring all your women.'

To her surprise, Jack let out a roaring laugh. 'You make it sound as though I have a harem. I don't, you know. In fact, at the moment I'm seeing no one but you.'

She didn't take him seriously. 'I bet you say that to all the girls. So, I guess the food must be the best if the great Jack Holden frequents the place.'

'It is.' He negotiated a few difficult corners, before saying, 'You've probably heard some rumours about me on the hospital grapevine.'

When she didn't answer he nodded and continued, 'I thought so. Don't believe everything you hear, Kathryn.' He paused for a moment before asking, 'Does everyone call you Kathryn? I know your brother calls you Kath.'

'Why? Don't you like it?'

'You know what I mean. I'm just curious. Kathryn definitely suits you but I—'

'My sister used to call me Katy but that was a long time ago and I just...' She shrugged. 'I guess I outgrew it.'

'You didn't mention you had a sister.'

'It's kind of complicated. She died a while ago.' Kathryn's tone was clipped.

'Want to talk about it?' he asked softly.

'No. Actually, I'd rather not,' she said decisively, and turned to look at him. 'Did anyone call you anything other than Jack?'

'Yes,' he said, a smile lighting his face. 'My brother has a few choice names. None of which are fit for lady's ears.'

Kathryn returned his smile, the sombre mood broken. When they arrived at the restaurant the rain was falling quite heavily. Jack told her to stay in the car while he quickly went to the boot and extracted a large, black umbrella.

They were met at the door by their hostess who was dressed in a kimono with chopsticks in her jet black hair. She bowed and said, '*Konnichi-wa.*' Kathryn bowed and returned the greeting. That was the extent of her Japanese.

Jack, on the other hand, began to rattle away in the language and after a moment the hostess gave a shy giggle, hiding behind her hand, at something he'd said. Their shoes were removed before they were shown to their table—a low table that required them to sit on the floor. Kathryn was thankful for the split in her dress which allowed her to manoeuvre to a comfortable position.

'Shall I order for you?' he asked, while the hostess waited patiently.

'Please,' Kathryn said. She looked around the dimly lit room with its elegantly simple decoration. The floor was tatami—rice matting—and the walls and sliding doors were rectangular wood frames covered with thin, pastel-painted paper. A few bonsai trees were placed in the corners. Apart from these and the low tables and small cushioned chairs, the room was empty.

'What do you think?' he asked as he watched her carefully.

'It's beautiful. Relaxing.' She turned and looked into his eyes. 'Thank you for bringing me here.'

'You're welcome,' he said with a smile, and raised her hand to his lips to brush a light kiss across it.

Kathryn felt her attraction toward Jack grow. Never had she imagined him to be so gentle or thoughtful. The fact that he was endeared him to her and *that* was something she'd rather didn't happen. He was already far too dangerous.

CHAPTER FIVE

THE food was brought out on flat black trays. Kathryn eyed the chopsticks their hostess gave her with dislike. She cleared her throat and smiled at the Japanese woman. 'Do you have a fork?'

'A fork?' Jack asked with amazement. 'Don't tell me the talented Dr Pearce can't eat with chopsticks. Can this be so?'

'It can,' she replied. 'Believe me, Jack, I've tried more than a thousand times, it seems, and they just don't work well with my fingers. Give me a scalpel any day.'

'But you don't eat with a scalpel,' he pointed out, and grinned as their hostess left to collect a fork for Kathryn. 'Just try it.'

She sighed and picked up the two wooden sticks. She placed them between her fingers as she'd been shown by numerous people on numerous occasions, each one intent on helping her combat her chopstick disability. Now it was obviously Jack's turn.

Holding them, she reached out for a piece of sushi and proceeded to chase it around the plate, disturbing the other bits of food and generally making a mess.

'You're right.' Jack chuckled as he gave into his mirth. 'Here...' He collected his own sticks, picked up a piece of food and held it to her lips. 'Allow me—or you'll die of starvation.'

Kathryn opened her mouth and accepted the food. She closed her lips around the chopsticks as Jack slowly withdrew them. Their eyes met and held for an electrifying instant. The act of him feeding her had been a completely innocent one, but somehow it had turned into a very sensual and erotic experience.

'We could do this all night,' he said softly, his voice threaded with desire. Kathryn chewed her food and swallowed, her eyes never breaking contact with his. It was as though only the two of them existed. Two pieces of a puzzle that fitted together perfectly.

'Your fork,' their hostess said as she knelt to serve them. She

65

poured the *sake*, before leaving them alone. Her timely interruption had broken the spell and after finding a mutual conversation point they talked softly for the next few hours.

On the drive home Kathryn put her head back against the head-rest and closed her eyes. 'It was a lovely meal. Thank you, Jack.'

'Are you trying to tell me you're ready to go home?' At his enquiring tone she opened her eyes.

'No. Why? Did you have something else in mind?'

'We could go raging all night at a dance club but...' He let his gaze sweep over her relaxed body sitting beside him. 'You don't look as though you have the energy. So why don't we...' he paused as he negotiated the corner '...go back to my town house and get warm in front of the fire?'

Kathryn knew the underlying meaning to his words and right then and there made up her mind to go for it. She was attracted to Jack Holden and had been dreaming about him ever since he'd rescued her on the ski slope.

He didn't press her but waited patiently for her answer. She knew she was probably doing the wrong thing. Getting involved with someone she worked closely with was a big no-no in her book, but the physical and emotional attraction she felt toward Jack won out in the end.

'I'd love to,' she replied, and closed her eyes again.

Neither spoke until Jack pulled the Jaguar off the road and garaged it beneath his town house. 'You awake?' he asked as he released his seat belt and leaned over.

'Yes,' she whispered, and reached out to run her fingers tenderly through his hair. Their lips met in fiery passion, both of them hungry, wanting and needing. Jack tried to draw her closer to him but found she was restricted by the seat belt.

Releasing it, he nibbled at her ear. 'Let's go inside. It's far too cramped in here.'

Once inside, Kathryn looked around his home and was more than impressed. It was tastefully decorated yet didn't show the tell-tale signs of an interior decorator.

'Coffee?' he asked, and Kathryn nodded. He walked off in

the direction of the kitchen, leaving her to browse around the dining and lounge rooms.

'Did you decorate this place yourself?' she asked loudly.

'No,' he replied. 'My sister did it. She's a decorator.'

Well, so much for her natural instinct, Kathryn thought. Although, if his sister had done it, she would know his likes and dislikes, thereby giving it the homey atmosphere it portrayed. She guessed that if she ever met his sister they'd probably get along quite well.

What was she thinking of? Hadn't Joan told her a few days ago that the women in Jack's life only lasted two to four weeks? She wouldn't be meeting his sister, or any other member of his family. She didn't even know where they lived.

Kathryn was still mentally berating herself for letting her foolish heart run away with her when Jack returned, carrying a tray ladened with coffee things.

'I didn't know how you took it so I have milk, cream and sugar. My mother trained me well, don't you think?'

'She did a great job.' Kathryn smiled. 'I take it black with no sugar. Sorry.'

'So do I. That means I've prepared and carried all this junk out here for nothing.'

'I guess it does,' she acknowledged as she went over to the fireplace. It was set up for the next blaze with wood, kindling and paper ready to light. Kathryn rubbed her arms, noticing that she was already quite warm.

'Do you have ducted heating?'

'Yes. Why? Are you cold?'

'No,' she replied. 'You probably don't need to light the fire at all.'

'But it adds to the atmosphere,' he said, and she smiled. She glanced at the two framed photographs on the mantelpiece. 'Your family?' she guessed as he handed her a cup of steaming coffee.

'Yes. This one...' he pointed to a photograph of him and his siblings '...was taken two years ago. Chris is in Queensland with Mum and Dad, and Rachael married last year and moved back to Melbourne. So I'm all alone here in South Australia.'

'You poor dear.' She feigned sympathy. 'And this one?' She pointed to the next photograph.

'All five of us, nearly eleven years ago.'

'That's *you*?' Kathryn asked, pointing to the man who had long hair and a long moustache and beard, standing between his parents.

'Yes. Didn't I look a sight? But that was the fashion in those days.'

Kathryn put her cup down on the coffee-table and reached for the photo. She'd seen a similar picture of him like that somewhere before. Perhaps there was one at the hospital that the staff had hung up as a joke. No. That wasn't it.

'What's wrong, Kathryn?' Jack asked when she continued to study the photo.

'Nothing,' she said with a frown. 'It's just that I've seen you like this somewhere before and I'm trying to remember where.' She sat down on the lounge and concentrated.

'Perhaps it was in a journal. I had a few papers published during med school and they usually have a photograph accompanying it.'

'No.' Kathryn shook her head as she closed her eyes. For some reason she recalled opening an envelope. A letter from Jill. It was a photograph that Jill had sent her. Jack had been in that photo. The realisation hit her. Jack had known Jill.

She looked up at him and he was instantly by her side. 'What's wrong, Kathryn? You've gone as white as a ghost.'

'Jill,' Kathryn whispered, and it was his turn to pale. 'Jill sent me a photograph of her medical friends in Africa.'

'You knew Jill?' Jack slumped to the floor.

'Yes.' Kathryn choked the word out. 'She was my sister.'

'Your sister?' he asked disbelievingly. 'Impossible. You don't even have the same surname. She couldn't possibly have been your sister.'

'It's true, Jack. Jill McKenna was my half-sister.' She knew she had Jack's attention, even though he was still staring out into space. 'Her father died when she was only a year old and our mother remarried two years later—my father. There were four years between us and Jill was the best big sister a girl could

ask for. We were very close.' Kathryn's voice broke and tears
began to fill her eyes. She'd never really shared anything about
Jill with an outsider—but, then, Jack, too, had known her, she
reminded herself.

Swallowing convulsively, Kathryn continued, 'Although Jill
didn't remember her father she still wanted to carry his name,
and my parents agreed. My mother, Bridgette, was a nurse and
married Patrick McKenna, a young medical intern, in a heated
rush. Jill was a honeymoon baby so they only had a few short
years together. My mother was devastated when he died. For
economic reasons she was forced to return to part-time nursing.

'She was fortunate enough to meet my father, who was also
a doctor, and he offered her a job running his private practice.
She was permitted to take Jill to work, which made life a lot
easier for her. Mitchell—that's my dad—took both of them into
his heart and soon found himself in love.

'I was born a year later and Steven came onto the scene seven
years after me. So for quite a while it was just Jill and myself.
She always wanted to be a doctor, like our fathers, and so we
used to play hospitals. She was the brilliant doctor and, of
course, because I was younger I was cajoled into being her
patient.' Kathryn looked off into the distance and smiled, for-
getting for a moment that she wasn't alone. 'We had some great
times.'

'You still miss her.' It was a statement, not a question, and
Kathryn lowered her watery eyes to look at Jack. His face was
as white as hers had been a few minutes ago.

'Yes. I do.' She was silent for a while, before saying quietly,
'Jack...how did you meet her?'

He was silent for so long that Kathryn thought he hadn't
heard her, but finally he said, 'We met at med school. Same
graduating class. Jill was bright, vivacious—so full of life. We
became good friends in our final year and spent a lot of time
studying together. You said you were close...didn't she ever
mention me?'

Kathryn smiled. Men! They always had to know what women
talked about. 'No, Jack. I was in my second year of med school
and too busy trying to follow in my brilliant sister's footsteps.'

She thought for a moment then said, 'She did mention she'd met someone who could teach her a lot. I suppose that could have been you.'

'Thank you. Very complimentary,' he said dryly. 'She was so dedicated. So driven. She knew exactly what she wanted to do and never once failed in her expectations. I was captivated by her.'

Kathryn felt a stirring of jealousy at Jack's words. The look on his face told her everything she needed to know. Jack had been in love with Jill. Any feelings Jack might have for her, Kathryn, would always be secondary to the ones he had had for Jill. She reined in her own emotions, holding them tight.

'I moved from Melbourne and did my internship here in Adelaide. We kept in loose contact and met up again a year later.'

Kathryn counted back the years. 'But that was when Jill went overseas to Africa.'

'I know,' Jack said solemnly as he rose to his feet. 'I went with her.' He picked up the photograph and returned it to the mantelpiece.

'To Africa?'

'Yes.'

'To work amongst the villagers?'

'Yes. I don't wish to discuss it any further.' His voice was sharp and held a distinct warning.

Kathryn knew she was pushing her limits but she had to ask. 'Were you in the same village as her?'

'I said I don't want to talk about it.'

Realisation dawned in Kathryn's eyes. 'You know what happened, don't you?' She stood up and looked him in the eye. 'You must tell me. My family needs to know.'

'Kathryn,' he said between clenched teeth.

'You can't do this to me, Jack,' she implored. 'We don't know what really happened. All we were told by the government was that a massacre had occurred and that everyone in the village had been killed.'

'Correct. I won't discuss it any further, Kathryn. I'm sorry.'

'Sorry!' Her voice rose and her temper flared. 'You *won't*

discuss it? That's not fair, Jack. We have a right to know, and if you're the only one who knows the truth then we need your help.'

'I don't know any more than you do,' he said harshly, his eyes murderous.

'You're lying,' Kathryn said accusingly. 'Who are you trying to protect? Why can't you tell me?' She knew she was bordering on the hysterical but couldn't stop herself.

Jack leapt to his feet and stormed over to the phone.

'What are you doing?' she asked.

'I'm calling you a taxi. If you can't let the subject drop I'd prefer you to leave.'

'I see,' she said icily, and collected her handbag. 'Don't bother. I'll walk home.'

'I can't let you do that,' he replied as he replaced the receiver, his anger under control.

'You don't own me, Jack. I can do what I like. If I choose to leave here and walk home, I will.'

'It's nearly midnight, Kathryn. Don't be foolish.'

'Stop treating me like a child,' she said between clenched teeth. 'It's only two blocks away and I've taken self-defence classes so you've fulfilled your obligations as a concerned friend.' She stormed over to the door and wrenched it open. 'Thank you for a very *enlightening* evening.'

He didn't call her name. He didn't come after her. Kathryn removed her shoes, not caring that the ground was wet and she'd probably catch a cold. At least the rain had stopped temporarily so she wouldn't get drenched.

Too many unasked questions had been definitely answered tonight. She'd wondered over the past few weeks what Jack saw in her. Was she just another conquest? Stupidly, she'd thought he enjoyed spending time with a woman who had a brain instead of the bimbos Joan had told her about.

Kathryn remembered what else Joan had told her. How Jack had been in love over ten years ago but the woman had died. Well, that was one hospital rumour that had been spot on. Jack hadn't been interested in her for herself. He'd been attracted because of her resemblance to Jill.

Kathryn knew she looked a lot like her sister but had always thought Jill to be much prettier. Perhaps it had been more Jill's self-confidence she'd admired. Jill, who had always been so full of life and energy. Always willing to meet new challenges head-on.

The Jill that Jack had loved. Had he hoped to resurrect his feelings for Jill through her? Playing second fiddle to her dead sister's memory was not something on which Kathryn wished to base a relationship.

She walked around the last corner and opened the gate that led to her front door. Jack's concern had not been necessary. She hadn't met a soul on her sad walk home. Fitting her key into the lock, she opened the door. A faint, flickering light was coming from the lounge room where Steven had fallen asleep in front of the TV.

He looked so sweet, sleeping with his head on the side. Like the little boy she remembered. He'd have a stiff neck if she didn't wake him. Kathryn flicked off the set, bringing her brother instantly to his feet.

'Kath! You're home.'

'Obviously.' She smiled at him, hoping he wouldn't see she was upset. She'd been gallantly holding back the tears until she reached the sanctity of her own room, but seeing Steven looking so young had brought too many memories flooding back.

'So how was the professor tonight? I hope he behaved himself.'

'He was a perfect gentleman,' Kathryn replied, but didn't elaborate. 'I'm tired and I'm going to bed. Night, Stevie.'

'Yeah. Goodnight, sis.'

Once Kathryn was safely behind her closed door she undressed, removed her make-up, brushed her teeth and dressed for bed. Taking the box of tissues with her, she climbed beneath the warm covers and let the tears begin to flow. They didn't stop for a long time.

Beep. Beep. Beep. Kathryn was pulled from sleep by the annoying sound. Perhaps it was Steven's pager and not hers, but discipline had taught her to always check—just in case. She unfolded her hand from the warm bed covers and reached out to grab the little black box off her bedside table. Pressing a button to illuminate the message, she discovered she was to call the hospital casualty department—immediately.

'Come on, Pearce,' she mumbled out loud. 'Wake up.' Glancing at the clock, she noted the time—eleven fifty-four p.m. She'd only been asleep for three hours and Kathryn felt positive her body needed a lot more than that to recover from her previous night's stint in Theatre.

She yawned and stretched in an attempt to wake up before switching on the light. After her eyes had adjusted she reached for her robe and slippers, then padded out into the cold hallway to the phone.

'Dr Pearce,' she said once the phone had been answered.

'We've got an orthopaedic emergency, Dr Pearce.' The sister's voice at the other end of the phone was brisk and to the point as she explained the trauma. 'A motor vehicle accident— both parents are undergoing surgery at Adelaide General Hospital and a small two-year-old boy has been brought in with multiple fractures.'

'I'll be there in fifteen minutes and I want all radiographs taken and ready for my perusal. Is there a theatre free?'

'Yes, Doctor.'

Kathryn spouted a few more requests before returning the receiver to its cradle. She was on her way back to her room when there was a noise at the front door. Ordinarily, she'd have been alarmed, but the phone call had put a multitude of scenarios in her head and concern for her small patient was top of the list.

A key was inserted into the lock and Kathryn realised it was her brother. Strange—she'd thought he was in bed. Steven materialised a few seconds later and received the shock of his life when he saw Kathryn standing in the hallway.

'Don't *do* that, Kath!' He placed a hand over his heart. 'I thought you were a burglar. What are you doing up?' he asked but his look told her he already knew the answer. 'Emergency?'

'Uh-huh.' She nodded, yawning again.

'Surely you're not on emergency call again?'

'Yes. Dr van der Merwe has taken leave and I've changed the roster so we're all doing a few extra shifts.'

'It's not fair. Knowing you, you've taken most of them.'

'Well, I'm the only one without a family so—'

'So you slog yourself into the ground. Why don't you discuss it with Professor Holden? Surely he can help find another ortho-pod to fill in on the roster?'

'It's my department, Steven. My responsibility. Really, I don't mind.' Kathryn shrugged off his words, not wanting to discuss *anything* with Jack regardless of how it was affecting her.

It had been two weeks since their Japanese dinner and the revelations that had followed. During that time they'd stayed out of each other's way unless absolutely necessary.

She returned to her room and Steven followed, obviously in-tent on once again making his point. 'You may be the only full-time orthopaedic surgeon on staff but the visiting surgeons have to do *some* work.'

'I can cope,' Kathryn said wearily, although she wasn't sure for how much longer.

'What's the emergency?' Steven asked softly as Kathryn fin-ished dressing.

'Two-year-old with multiple fractures—MVA. Parents are in Adelaide General Hospital, having their fair share of theatre time, I presume.'

'Can I help?'

'No. Get some sleep. You'll be on my orthopaedic rotation next week and then you'll be begging me for some time off.' She ran a brush through her hair before braiding it. She looked at her brother and took in his attire. 'Where have you been dressed up like a penguin?'

'Charity bash over at the Hyatt for a children's hostel. Quite a few of the staff were there, including your new nemesis, Professor Holden. And let me tell you, Kath, he had quite a dish on his arm. What a beauty!'

'Steven,' she said sharply, a pang of jealousy sparking through her body. 'That's no way to talk about another human being and, quite frankly, I don't have time to stay here and discuss Professor Holden's love life with you.' She grabbed her purse and car keys before stalking out of the room.

The roads were wet and the night held a distinct chill. No wonder there had been a spate of car accidents. There were always more during the winter months.

'There you are, Dr Pearce.' A uniformed sister came up to her and ushered her towards a cubicle. 'He's in here, poor dear.' They went in and Kathryn looked down at the small child. Her heart constricted with grief at such a sight. He was battered and bruised, probably from being thrown around the car.

'Where's my registrar?' she asked quietly as she held out her hand for the boy's chart.

'He's on his way. I've just sent word that you've arrived. We've had a six-year-old girl in with a broken arm and I believe Dr Harris is just finishing her cast.'

Kathryn nodded her acknowledgment and continued reading the chart. His name was Joel Brooks and his birthdate indicated he was two and a half. 'How come we have so many details about him if his parents are unconscious?'

'An emergency medical kit, found in the car, contained a copy of a child identification form. It listed all his particulars, allergies, medications and so on. It's made our job a lot easier and the next of kin has been notified. I wish more parents were as organised as little Joel's.'

Kathryn sighed. 'I agree. Now, do I have some X-rays to view? It says here that he's fractured his right arm and right tibia.'

'That's correct, Dr Pearce,' Dr Harris replied as he entered the cubicle.

'Has he regained consciousness at all?'

'No. One of the main reasons I had you paged was because I noticed a fracture to his skull when we were cleaning him up. When the X-rays came back...' Dr Harris reached into a large packet, withdrew a radiograph and held it to the light '...there was a small hairline fracture only slightly visible. I've ordered a CAT scan and he's due to be taken up to Radiology once you've examined him.'

'So,' Kathryn said once she'd reviewed the other radiographs.

'We're looking at inserting screws into the ulna...' she pointed to his arm '...and possibly plating his skull.' She took a closer look at the tibia. 'We can't put a plaster cast on his shin because of the open cuts so please have an external fixator ready.' She shook her head. 'Poor little chap.'

They were soon on their way to Radiology for the computerised axial tomography scan and Kathryn was glad little Joel was still unconscious. All this technology was overwhelming to adults, let alone children. Once the scan was completed, Kathryn went to the doctors' lounge for a much-needed cup of coffee. When the results were ready Dr Harris brought them down and together they reviewed their findings.

'That looks like a tumour to me,' Kathryn said, shaking her head in despair. 'He's only two.' She stared at the radiographs for a moment longer, hoping to change the diagnosis. 'Book him in for an MRI scan immediately.'

Dr Harris gulped. 'Magnetic resonance imaging is very expensive, Dr Pearce. Perhaps you should get a neurosurgeon's opinion, before ordering it.'

Kathryn took a deep breath. 'I'd like the MRI done immediately, Dr Harris,' she said firmly, and this time he nodded, before scurrying away to organise the scan.

The MRI proved she was correct. It was a tumour. Kathryn was silent for a moment before she turned to Dr Harris who was standing meekly behind her. 'Contact Professor Holden immediately. I need him in for a consultation on the status of that tumour.'

'But he's not on call tonight.'

'I don't care. I want him here in the hospital in less than half an hour. I need to operate on that little boy and I have to know more about what's going on around his brain.'

'I should warn you, Dr Pearce, that Professor Holden doesn't take kindly to his evenings being interrupted.'

Kathryn rounded on her registrar, her eyes blazing with temper. 'If he doesn't want to have his evenings interrupted then he should choose another profession. He was at a charity function at the Hyatt earlier tonight so you shouldn't have any trouble tracking him down if he doesn't have his mobile phone with him. Now do it!'

A pale Dr Harris left the doctors' lounge as Kathryn sank back into the chair. That would teach him to question her decisions.

It was precisely twenty-two minutes later that the door opened again and Kathryn looked up from the medical journal she was reading to see Professor Jack Holden in the doorway, looking devastatingly handsome in his black tuxedo.

Her mouth went dry, her palms began to sweat and she was grateful to be sitting down as she was sure her knees would have gone weak. Damn him. He could still evoke such a powerful response within her, just by walking into a room. She'd never seen him in a tux but now she had the memory would plague her for ever. Kathryn breathed deeply in an attempt to get her body under control as she stood to face him.

'What do you mean by interrupting my evening?' he thundered, and for one split second she wondered whether she'd bitten off more than she could chew.

His angry words whisked away the mushy emotions she'd experienced, replacing them with her own anger. This was the first time they'd been alone since that night in his apartment— and both of them knew it.

Her eyes burned as she said firmly, 'I had you paged because I have a neurosurgical case for you to look at.' Professionalism. That was the only avenue of communication they had left.

'I'm not on call. What if I had been out on the town? Drinking? It is my night off so why shouldn't I enjoy myself?'

She swallowed her anger, knowing that what he said was correct but also that if she aggravated him any further he might just leave—and she needed him.

'You're correct and I apologise, Professor.'

He raised an eyebrow at her words then said more quietly, 'Why didn't you contact Dr Brahms?'

'Because I feel this boy needs the best and I've been told by nearly every member of staff that the best is you.'

'You sound as though you don't believe them,' he taunted as

he relaxed against the doorframe. His eyes travelled the length of her body, taking in the tracksuit and running shoes she wore.

Kathryn tilted her chin at his open appraisal and her eyes dared him to comment on her attire. She pointed to his jacket. 'Why don't you take off your dinner jacket and come see him?' That way she'd hopefully find him less appealing. She forced herself to concentrate on the job at hand. 'His name is Joel and he's only two and a half. MVA—parents are in Adelaide General Hospital, undergoing surgery.'

She levelled her gaze at him and said imploringly, 'Once you've seen him, Jack, you'll know what I'm talking about.'

He removed his jacket and threw it over a chair, then leaned back against the doorframe. He was blocking the doorway and when Kathryn indicated that she wanted to pass he merely turned side-on. She was forced to squeeze her way past and try as she might not to come into contact with him it was inevitable. Her breasts brushed lightly across his warm chest and her eyes flew up to meet his. Her body came to life—a life she'd denied it for two long weeks. Jack lifted his hand and ran it down her cheek. She knew her desire was evident in her eyes.

'Ditto!' he whispered huskily.

It was enough to break the spell and Kathryn turned away. Clearing her throat, she led the way to their small patient. Never in her life had she been more aware of the sway of her hips. Although she tried to make her natural stride less provocative, she knew it didn't work. All the way to the cubicle she could feel Jack's eyes roving over her body. She could imagine his fingers running lightly over her, caressing every inch—knowing her more intimately than any other man.

Exhaling steadily, Kathryn fought for control, and when they reached the small room she lowered her gaze and stood aside for Jack to precede her.

'Has he stirred at all?' he asked the nurse who was sitting beside the bed.

'Yes, Professor. A few moments before you walked in. I was about to send for Dr Pearce—' She broke off as a soft whimper came from Joel. 'It's all right, little man,' the nurse soothed.

'Analgesics?' Jack asked, and Kathryn handed him the chart.

'Pethidine, but it should be wearing off. I'd like to get him anaesthetised as soon as possible so I can attend to his orthopaedic injuries, but I need your opinion on the scans.' As she spoke she hooked the scan onto the viewing box for Jack to look at.

'*You* ordered an MRI?' he asked with surprise.

'Obviously,' she replied, and pointed to the scan.

'You were very sure of your diagnosis. MRIs cost this hospital quite a lot of money. You should have waited for my opinion on the CAT scans, before investigating further.'

'That may be so, Professor Holden,' Kathryn whispered fiercely, 'but as the admitting orthopaedic surgeon and Acting Director of the orthopaedic department, I consider it my duty to my patients to perform *all* necessary tests—regardless of cost— to ensure they get the correct treatment. I need to take Joel to Theatre as soon as possible. In my opinion, my actions were correct. I don't see the point in quibbling about such trivial matters as hospital costs when this little boy's life is at stake.'

The nurse gasped at Kathryn's words. It was becoming increasingly apparent that no one, regardless of position, spoke to the great Jack Holden in such a fashion. Kathryn waited almost flinchingly for his reply but he merely nodded and took a closer look at the scans. He studied them for a quite a while, before turning back to Kathryn.

'Definitely a tumour. There should be no added trauma in taking him to Theatre now.'

'Good,' Kathryn replied, and turned to the nurse. 'Please contact Dr Harris and have him arrange Theatre immediately.' She waited for the nurse to leave before she looked at Jack. 'Thank you for coming in...' Now she was beginning to regret her outburst over the scans. 'I really do appreciate it and I'm sorry to have spoilt your evening.'

Jack stood with his hands deep in his pockets. His eyes narrowed and a hint of a smile played around his lips. 'As much as I deserved your tirade, do you now have the audacity to dismiss me, Kathryn?'

'Well...I thought that...' she stammered, unsure how to react.

'You've called me into the hospital for a very sick little boy and I'm not about to leave. I'll be in Theatre with you—just in case any complications arise.' He stared down at her and the look in his eyes caused Kathryn to tingle with anticipation. She could tell he wanted to kiss her and at that moment she couldn't think of anything she wanted more. Slowly, a knowing grin covered his face and Kathryn could have kicked herself for letting him get under her skin. He knew darned well the conflicting emotions he was causing and he liked it.

Kathryn pulled herself together and broke eye contact, her face flushed. 'Let's get the ball rolling.' She turned and walked out of the cubicle ahead of him, almost colliding with Dr Harris in her haste to leave.

'I received your message, Dr Pearce,' he said, and she saw him glance briefly over her shoulder. When he realised the professor was no longer in a bad mood he breathed a sigh of relief and returned his attention to Kathryn.

'I've organised for the external fixator to be autoclaved so if we could begin with the ulna the sterilisation should be complete by the time we're ready to fix the tibia.'

'Fine. I'll be in the change rooms if anyone needs me.' As Kathryn turned on her heel to leave there was a commotion at the sister's desk.

'Where is he? I demand to see him.' The shrill feminine voice belonged to a stunningly beautiful blonde, dressed in a tight-fitting red dress that clung the length of her long, nubile body. Diamonds adorned her ears, neck and wrist. Long black gloves reached to just below her shoulder where a fur coat, probably mink, lay protectively around her.

'It's all right.' Jack came forward and took the lady's hand. 'I'm sorry, Veronica, but I'm needed in Theatre.'

Looking at the beautiful woman again, Kathryn couldn't help the feelings of complete dislike and jealousy that swamped her. Veronica looked breathtaking, as though she'd stepped out of the latest glossy magazine, while Kathryn felt tackily dressed in her comfortable tracksuit. She shook her head in disgust and brought her thoughts back to order. Only seconds ago Jack had been flirting with her while Veronica was waiting for him. How dared he!

'What am I supposed to do?' Veronica said. 'I can't very well go back to the charity ball without an escort.'

'Of course not,' Kathryn whispered sarcastically to Dr Harris, who raised his eyebrows in surprise at her sharp tongue. 'She was born to decorate someone's arm. She'd look almost lop-sided if a man wasn't there to prop her up.' The green-eyed monster was on the prowl and she couldn't control it.

'I said I was sorry, Veronica, but it can't be helped. I'm needed here,' Jack said indulgently, as though he were talking to a small child.

Realising her ploy wasn't working, Veronica switched tactics and slid a hand up his arm and around his neck. 'But, Jack,' she said, and pulled a pouting face, her voice as sweet as honey, 'I need you, too. Can't someone else operate or whatever it is you do? You're not even supposed to be working tonight so I don't think it's very fair.'

'Oh, please,' Kathryn said, and Dr Harris chuckled.

'I'm a doctor, Veronica,' he explained patiently. 'Now I'll walk you back to the limo and call you tomorrow.'

'I'm out of here.' Kathryn threw her hands in the air and walked away from the stomach-churning scene. How could Jack be interested in such a bimbo? Is that all a woman was to him—a decoration to be pacified? Joan had warned her but she'd thought that after what had happened between them... No. She wouldn't think about that tonight. Jack and her sister and their relationship were to be wiped from her mind. Little Joel needed her undivided attention and he was going to get it. She collected her theatre clothes and entered the change rooms, but the green-eyed monster wouldn't be put to rest so easily.

'I need you too. It's just not fair.' Kathryn mimicked Veronica's voice perfectly. She pulled a face in the mirror and turned to her locker. What had Steven called her? A dish! Yeah, a dish of baloney. Perhaps Jack preferred baloney all wrapped up in a red package but Kathryn knew that a woman—*the* woman—for Jack Holden would have to stimulate him intellectually as well as physically.

Want to apply for the job? a little voice inside her head asked. Yes, her heart answered immediately. She eyed herself critically in the mirror, looking at her features. Undoing the long plait, Kathryn let her hair hang loose. She reached into her locker and pulled out her brush.

Giving it a quick once-over, she reassessed her image. Much more seductive, she thought. She struck a pose similar to Veronica's pouting one and realised she looked as ghastly as the other woman had. Did men really find it attractive?

'Kathryn!' Jack's voice echoed into the ladies' change room. Immediately she dropped her silly pose, her heart pounding wildly at the thought of being caught admiring herself.

'Kathryn,' he bellowed again, and this time she heard footsteps, coming toward her. When Jack rounded the row of lockers where Kathryn was he stopped and stared at her, the severe expression sliding off his face.

'Your hair...' Slowly he walked over to her and raised his hand to run his fingers gently through the loose strands. 'I told you I liked it long, but it's even better loose.'

Kathryn was mesmerised by his touch. His other hand came up to cup her face. 'You're lovely.' He bent his head and claimed her lips in an earth-shattering kiss. She closed her eyes and gave herself up to him. This was what she'd wanted for the past few weeks—to be back in Jack's arms where she felt she belonged.

Pulling away, Jack looked down at her. 'I've missed you.' He gathered her to him, resting her head against his chest. They stood together for a few minutes before Kathryn craned her neck to look at him.

'Have you missed me—or Jill?'

Jack abruptly let her go as though she'd burnt him. 'That's a cheap shot, Kathryn.'

'Is it? How do you expect me to react when you won't tell me what happened?'

'Do you really need to know?'

'If we're going to have any kind of successful relationship— yes. I think it would be a very important factor.'

'Do you want me to confess all my previous lovers—my re-lationship with Veronica? My past is *my* past, Kathryn, and whether that involves your sister or not the memories belong to me and I will not discuss them.'

'Why not? I don't understand,' she yelled at him, throwing up her hands in exasperation.

He clenched his fists and glared at her angrily. 'If you were a man I'd hit you.'

'Go ahead,' Kathryn retorted. 'Don't let the simple fact that I'm a woman stop your primal urges.' She stuck out her chin and closed her eyes tightly. Seconds later she was being hauled against him and punishingly kissed.

Releasing her, Jack said stonily, 'Jill was part of my past. You're just going to have to accept it and be satisfied.' With that, he turned on his heel and walked out of the room.

CHAPTER SIX

KATHRYN met with Dr Harris and reviewed the X-rays, before talking over the technique she was going to use. Soon their little patient was anaesthetised and ready for the operation to begin.

There was no sign of Jack, and Kathryn briefly wondered whether Veronica had won in the end. No. She dismissed the thought. Jack might have certain flaws but where his patients were concerned he was extremely reliable.

She was scrubbing when she felt rather than saw him walk in. Her body tingled and the hairs on her arms stood on end.

'Don't scrub too hard, Dr Pearce. You need *some* flesh left on your arms,' he said softly into her ear, and goosebumps spread over her body. Kathryn refused to turn her head, knowing if she did their lips would be too close for comfort. She looked straight ahead and focused on the task of removing grime and dirt from her hands.

Jack didn't scrub and stood back, simply observing her work. This was the first time he'd been in Theatre with her and, after taking a deep breath, Kathryn expelled the nerves he'd induced.

'All right, Dr Harris,' she told her assistant, 'let's get this ulna fixed.' Kathryn made the incision and, with Dr Harris's help, retracted the skin and muscles. She lifted her head and glanced at the opposite wall where the X-rays of Joel's arm were illuminated for her to see. Jack was standing just to the left of them and she fought hard not to let her eyes stray towards him.

She returned her attention to the patient. 'Suction, please,' she said softly. Her gloved hands worked steadily and competently as she fixed the bone together with a metal plate and screws.

After a check X-ray had been taken and she'd pronounced herself satisfied, she began to close the wound in layers. As she tied the last knot the external fixator was brought into Theatre directly from the autoclave.

'Nice timing,' she murmured to the nurse who'd brought it through. Again, she could see Jack in her peripheral vision when she looked at the nurse but refused to allow her eyes to look directly at him. Every nerve was zinging in her body because of his close proximity.

Focus on your patient, she instructed herself sternly. She looked down at Joel's leg. His open wounds had been cleaned expertly and his small leg was looking much better. Checking the X-rays once more, she marked the correct position for the pins to be inserted into his bone. The fixator included ring fixation and the intricacies of the technique took the next hour to complete.

When she was finished Joel's leg looked like something akin to that of a robot. Why couldn't they make these devices in different colours? she thought as she stood back to admire her handiwork. It was a rhetorical question and one to which she knew the answer. She exhaled on a deep sigh, before turning to thank her team.

'Good work, everyone. Thank you for your assistance.' She let her gaze slide around the room, meeting everyone's eyes. She was ready now—ready to meet Jack's eyes—but when she looked for him he wasn't to be found. He must have slipped out in the past few moments when she'd been absorbed in the final adjustments of the fixator.

A feeling of disappointment swamped her as she went to the changing rooms. Under the hot spray of the shower, Kathryn acknowledged that she was eagerly awaiting some praise from Jack. She'd expected him to wait until the end of the operation and then cross to her and congratulate her on a job well done. But he hadn't. He hadn't even stayed until the end.

She swallowed a lump in her throat and fiercely pushed back the tears that threatened to spill over. Why should she feel such desolation because Jack hadn't remarked on her skills? Because his opinion of her mattered far too much.

As she dressed she pulled her thoughts back into line and concentrated on important matters, such as Joel's recovery. They would watch how he responded to this treatment in the next twenty-four hours, and if everything went according to plan Jack would perform the tumour removal the day after tomorrow. Kathryn had already decided to stand in at that operation, even though she'd heard that Jack didn't allow spectators into his theatre. He'd done it to her so she'd do it to him, she thought, and gave herself a satisfied nod at the idea.

When she strapped her watch to her wrist she saw that it was a quarter to six in the morning. At the same moment her stomach grumbled, and she decided that breakfast was her next priority. Going to Recovery, she checked on Joel, who was still sedated, before she walked up the road from the hospital to a quiet café. As she went she bumped into Dr Harris, who seemed to heading in the same direction.

'Hungry?' she asked, giving him a smile. He hesitated, before returning her smile and nodding. 'Would you like to join me for breakfast?' Kathryn waited for his reply and tried not to get impatient at his hesitation. They'd reached the café door when he reluctantly agreed.

Kathryn laughed. 'I'm not trying to force anything on you, Dr Harris. I'm hungry—you're hungry. Let's sit at the same table and eat some food—perhaps even share in a little conversation. That's all. I promise.'

He appeared happier after her speech and when they'd ordered he waited for Kathryn to say something. 'I noticed on your hospital identification badge that your first initial is "A". What does it stand for?'

'Andrew—but most of my friends call me Andy.'

He was extremely shy, Kathryn realised, and tried to put him at ease. 'Do you mind if I call you Andy? I'd prefer it if you called me Kathryn.'

He nodded. 'I know we're supposed to use first names around the children but it feels disrespectful. Until I'm asked to call someone—especially a consultant—by their first name, I generally use titles.'

'Well, that's settled, then,' Kathryn said as her breakfast of scrambled eggs, bacon, toast and coffee was placed in front of her. 'Fantastic!' she told the waitress, and began to eat.

'You weren't kidding when you said you were hungry,' Andy said with a chuckle. They chatted between mouthfuls about how they thought the operation had gone and general hospital matters. Kathryn discovered that Andy was due to sit his final exams in another eighteen months and was about to begin his study regime.

'I know all about it,' she groaned. 'I only officially finished my training a few months ago. This is my first position as a consultant.'

'Really?' He seemed amazed. 'You're so sure of yourself. You know exactly what you want and appear so confident.'

'Everyone's fallible,' she replied. 'I accepted this position to see if I could cope with being Acting Director. So far it appears to be going well.'

'I'll say,' Andy agreed.

'I have my doubts,' said another deep voice from beside them, and they both looked up at Jack. 'Mind if I join you?'

Kathryn looked over at Andy who had shrunk back into his shell. Not waiting for an answer, Jack pulled out a chair and sat down.

'Any suggestions on what to eat?' He glanced at Kathryn's half-empty plate. 'That looks good.' He signalled for the waitress and gave his order.

Andy put his knife and fork together and stood to leave. 'I'd better get back,' he said.

Kathryn didn't want to be left alone with Jack so she reached out and pulled Andy down again. 'You can't go yet,' she said sweetly. 'You haven't finished. After such a long evening in Casualty and then in Theatre you need all the sustenance you can get.'

Jack chuckled, indicating he knew what she was doing.

'No, really,' Andy said, clambering up again. 'I'm quite full and I'd better be getting back to the hospital to check on the patients.'

'I'm your boss, Andy, and I think you need some time away from the hospital. I know how hard training registrars work so stay. Have another coffee—my treat.' Kathryn tried to persuade him as she noticed Andy's eyes darting like a scared rabbit between Jack and herself.

Andy's beeper sounded and he breathed an audible sigh,

thankful the decision had been taken out of his hands. He opened his mouth to say something as Kathryn and Jack looked at him expectantly but closed it again, gave them both a brief nod and almost ran out of the café.

'Don't worry,' Kathryn grumbled. 'I'll pay.'

'That's what you get for asking a preoccupied registrar out to breakfast.'

'I didn't ask him out to breakfast,' she retorted. 'I asked him to join me. Until we sat down, I didn't even know his first name.'

'It's in the files I gave you,' Jack said as he ate his food. 'Now, why don't you finish off your breakfast? I know you're hungry.' He raised his eyebrows and winked at her. How did he always manage to take an innocent remark and turn it into some kind of sexual invitation—an invitation Kathryn was all too willing to accept?

'You operate very...decisively,' Jack said between mouthfuls.

'What's that supposed to mean?' Kathryn shot back.

'Nothing. It was supposed to be a compliment.'

'Are you sure you know *how* to give compliments, Jack? I thought it was a field of expertise you'd flunked.'

'You're still mad at me, aren't you?' he said, and Kathryn gritted her teeth.

'Whatever gave you that impression?' she replied sweetly. She finished off her food and pushed her plate away. 'Well, I hate to eat and run but I've got things to do, places to go and people not to see.' She drained her cup and stood. Jack clamped one hand around her wrist to stop her walking away.

'Have dinner with me.'

He didn't even ask her, Kathryn thought. It was a command she had no say in. She looked down into his blue eyes and felt her heart begin to soften. No doubt both her heart and her body would betray her if she said yes so she squared her shoulders and tried not to think about the wonderful sensations he evoked when he kissed her, before saying firmly, 'No.' She wrenched her wrist free of his grasp and walked away from the table.

When she got to the door she turned back to look at him. He had been staring at her rear, and his eyes flicked up almost guiltily to meet hers. 'By the way, thanks for breakfast. From both Dr Harris and myself.'

On the short walk back to the hospital Kathryn replayed the conversation in her mind. If Jack had asked, rather than ordered, her to have dinner with him, she might have relented. He was such an arrogant pig that she felt he deserved to be put in his place. No doubt, women like Veronica were willing to fall all over him at his merest suggestion but not her. Kathryn decided she owed it to herself to teach Jack Holden a lesson.

She checked on Joel, who'd been taken to Intensive Care and was in a satisfactory condition, before collecting some papers from her office. There was no sign of Andy Harris and Kathryn assumed he'd either gone home or was stuck in Casualty again.

She grinned to herself as she dumped the paperwork into her car and headed for home. Poor Dr Harris. She wondered what his reaction had been when he'd realised he'd left his consultant surgeon to pay for his breakfast—if he'd realised at all. Just wait until she told him that Professor Holden had paid. The poor registrar was so caught up with hospital hierarchy and policy that he couldn't appreciate people for who they were.

On Sunday Kathryn went to the hospital to review Joel Brooks. His grandmother was by his side in the intensive care unit. Kathryn stood back and watched as the concerned woman held his small hand in hers. Not wanting to intrude on the moment, Kathryn checked his nursing notes and discussed what his condition had been during the night.

'Professor Holden telephoned a while ago to say he was on his way in. Mrs Paris—that's Joel's grandmother—has been here ever since the sun came up,' the ward sister informed her. 'Apparently, she and her husband are torn between spending time with their daughter and son-in-law and their only grandson. Just as well the two hospitals are close.'

Kathryn shook her head at the turn of events. 'How are Mr and Mrs Brooks doing?'

'Both stable in Intensive Care. We've been keeping in close contact with Adelaide General Hospital, which has alleviated some of the parents' concern.'

'What were their injuries?'

'Mr Brooks has fractured both his legs, his right arm and quite a few ribs. He received a bad concussion when his head hit the steering-wheel but, fortunately, no brain damage.'

Kathryn winced. 'And Mrs Brooks?'

'Luckier than her husband. Fractured both arms, a few ribs and received a minor concussion. Both have bad whiplash but that goes without saying with motor vehicle accidents.'

'If Jack's coming in then I'll wait and we can review Joel together. No point in disturbing him more than necessary.'

'Good thinking,' Jack said, obviously overhearing Kathryn's words as he walked into the ward sister's office. 'Status?'

'He vomited an hour ago and your registrar gave him another dose of Maxolon to stop it. Temperature and blood pressure are up. Orthopaedic injuries are satisfactory. Second pin site of external fixator is slightly inflamed but nothing that can't be controlled.'

Kathryn had partially listened to the sister's report, while trying to calm her frantic heartbeat. Why did he have to affect her in such a way? Why couldn't she control herself? She took a deep breath and felt more steady.

'Right,' Jack said. 'Let's review him.'

Kathryn followed him over to where Mrs Paris sat, talking quietly to her grandson. After introducing both Kathryn and himself, Jack asked after Joel's parents. Mrs Paris gave a watery smile before answering.

'Picking up nicely, the doctors have said. My poor Abigail just wants to see her son.' She stroked her grandson's hair. 'I think it would do him the world of good as well.'

'I know,' Jack agreed, 'but, unfortunately, Joel is too sick to be moved. It's best if we can all keep a positive outlook and know that in a few days they can probably see each other.'

'Yes,' Mrs Paris said, wringing a handkerchief in her hands.

'I'll be going over to Adelaide General Hospital this afternoon to see your daughter and son-in-law. I've already explained the operation to Abigail but I promised to go over it again after she'd had some time to think about it.'

Mrs Paris dabbed at her eyes with her hanky and asked in a wavering voice, 'What's wrong with him, Professor Holden?'

Jack asked the ward sister to bring over the scans so he could explain things to Joel's grandmother.

'According to the scans we've done, Joel has what we call a dermoid tumour. It's basically an ingrown hair that's grown inside and outside the skull—connected together.' He hooked the scans onto a nearby viewer and they all crowded around.

'Does it have to come out? I've read somewhere that some brain tumours are better off left in,' Mrs Paris asked hopefully.

'It definitely needs to come out, Mrs Paris. If you look here...' he pointed to the tumour '...it's pressing on the cerebellum which is the lower part of the brain. The cerebellum is responsible for things like posture, balance and fine movement.'

'I guess that would explain why he was always falling down and losing his balance. Why, you could hardly walk past him without him falling down. He'd also been vomiting quite a lot. My daughter's general practitioner diagnosed it as a tummy bug. Gastro...' She faltered over the medical term.

'Gastroenteritis?' Jack queried as he made a note of the information Mrs Paris had just given him. 'The symptoms for a head injury are nausea and vomiting, accompanied by headaches which can often turn into migraines. These symptoms can also be related to gastroenteritis. As for the loss of balance, that's a definite sign of a tumour but can also be attributed to ear infections as well. Unless Abigail had given him all the information about Joel's condition—some of which she may not have felt was relevant—then the doctor would look for the most common problem and solution.

'But for now we need to know any details of Joel's life, regardless of how irrelevant they may seem to you. When you think of something tell the nursing staff, who'll make a note of it.'

'I'll do what I can,' Mrs Paris replied. She almost seemed relieved at being able to help. 'But what about that...contraption on his leg and what about his arm?'

Kathryn stepped forward and smiled at Mrs Paris. 'It's fine for Professor Holden to operate. Joel's orthopaedic injuries are healing nicely but if there's anything you need to have explained to you just say so and I'll go over it, although I think for the moment you've probably digested enough information.'

'Thank you both,' she replied with a smile. 'It's a comfort to know he's in such capable hands.'

Considering Joel was sleeping peacefully, Kathryn had a quick look at his fixator site and agreed with the ward sister's diagnosis and treatment plan. She and Jack left Intensive Care and walked the short block to Adelaide General Hospital to see his parents.

Abigail Brooks not only had her son to worry about but her husband as well, and Kathryn's heart went out to her. She looked pale, except for the bruises on her face, as she lay back amongst the white hospital sheets.

Jack once again took charge and reported on Joel's present condition with the help of the X-rays and scans. Abigail had quite a few questions which Jack answered, making sure she comprehended the medical intricacies. The emotional pain evident in her eyes was mixed with a determination to get through this trying and, at times, frustrating ordeal.

'It's amazing. If we hadn't had that accident, Joel's tumour might not have been discovered until it was too late,' she said.

'Signs and symptoms have probably been there from the beginning but no one knew to look further than the obvious. Your mother told me he'd been diagnosed with gastroenteritis.'

Abigail nodded. 'He was hospitalised just after his first birthday because of it. We went to the hospital closer to our home and he was in for three nights. The vomiting stopped so they discharged him.'

'Most of the symptoms of this particular tumour are similar to gastro but we've diagnosed it now and we'll be doing everything we can tomorrow. I'll call you the second I'm out of Theatre. That's a promise.'

'Thank you—for everything. It's good to know Joel has such nice people looking after him.'

'You concentrate on getting yourself better and in a few days' time we should be able to take you over in a wheelchair to see him,' Kathryn said with a smile before they left her in peace.

'It's so heart-wrenching,' she said to Jack as they walked back to their hospital.

'I know,' he agreed, and placed his arm around her waist. It was comfort he was offering, and it was precisely what Kathryn needed.

'I have to stop by and see Chantal McBain before I head on home,' Kathryn said when they reached the hospital grounds. Then an idea dawned. She smiled sweetly at Jack. 'Would you mind coming with me? I think you might be of some use.'

'In what way?' Jack's curiosity was piqued. 'Is she a bad patient?'

'On the contrary, she's more than happy to do any exercises to strengthen her knee, she's coping well with her arm in plaster and her toes are healing nicely. The problem is with her appearance.'

'What's wrong with it? When I saw her in Casualty she looked like a very attractive girl.'

'She is.' Kathryn turned into the corridor and walked beside Jack to the orthopaedic ward. 'Chantal feels her physical appearance has changed since the accident. Looks are very important in those teenage years. Mrs. McBain told me Chantal had planned on entering a teen beauty contest in a few months' time, but now she doesn't think she stands a chance.'

'But her bruises and grazes will be gone by then.'

'I know that,' Kathryn stressed, 'you know that and her parents know that. Unfortunately, Chantal's self-confidence has taken a dramatic dive and we need to boost it before she sinks into depression.'

'What about her knee? That won't be ready in a few months.'

'She doesn't seem to consider that an obstacle for this contest. I guess it's the facial looks that are of high importance in these beauty pageants.'

'So you'd like me to come and help boost her morale.'

'Her parents have tried and so have I. We've told her that true beauty comes from within and there will be other contests to enter.' Kathryn shook her head sadly. 'She finally broke down and confessed her reason for desperately wanting to enter this particular contest. Basically it's peer group pressure—you know how bad *that* can be during these trying years. She feels that by entering the contest she will be proving her worth to the girls applying the pressure.'

Jack nodded. 'You're hoping I can supply a different perspective, not only as another doctor but a man.'

'Got it in one.' Kathryn smiled as they walked past the nurses' desk.

'Which room is she in?' he asked, straightening his tie and making sure his shirt was tucked in.

'Twelve.' Kathryn led the way and knocked briefly on the closed door, before pushing it open and walking in.

'Hello,' she said to Chantal, who was lying back amongst the pillows, flicking idly through a teen magazine.

'Hi,' she managed but didn't raise her eyes. Mrs McBain, who was sitting in the chair beside the bed, shrugged.

'How's the knee?' Kathryn asked Chantal.

'Good.'

This was the way it had been for the past few days. Monosyllables only. Kathryn gave the bandaged knee a cursory glance, before introducing Jack.

'I'd like you to meet a friend of mine,' she said.

'Sure.' Chantal kept turning the pages, hardly seeing them at all.

'Hello, Chantal.' Jack's deep masculine voice penetrated the haze around the teenager.

The girl's baby-blue eyes flicked up to meet his. 'Wh-who are you?'

'I'm Jack,' he supplied as he moved a few magazines to the foot of her bed, before gently sitting on the edge. 'I was in Casualty when you were brought in and wanted to come by and see how you were feeling.'

His tone was so caring, so sincere, that Kathryn knew he would get through to her. Chantal's eyes dipped to the magazine for a brief second before she lifted them once again to meet his.

'Actually,' she said in a small voice, 'I'm not doing too good.'

'What's the problem?'

As far as Chantal was concerned, there was no one in the

room but herself and Jack. Mrs McBain was sitting very still in her chair, as though not wanting to frighten away her daughter's first impulse to talk.

'I'm scarred.' The words were said with choked-up emotion and within another second the flood gates opened. Kathryn watched as Jack instinctively moved forward to tenderly embrace the girl before him.

Chantal buried her face in his shoulder and sobbed. Kathryn's eyes met Mrs McBain's who nodded and smiled, her own eyes filled with unshed tears. Reaching for the tissues, Kathryn held a few out to Jack who took them and offered them to Chantal.

When her sobs finally receded into small hiccups Jack pulled back and looked at her face. 'Do you think these cuts and bruises make you look ugly?' he asked softly. Chantal nodded. 'Then you're wrong.' Those last three words were said with such conviction that Chantal turned to look at her mother.

'He's right, darling. You're not ugly.'

'You couldn't be if you tried,' Jack said with a smile. He reached out and brushed a tear from her cheek. 'Kathryn tells me you plan to enter a beauty contest in a few months' time. Why don't you tell me about it?'

'I...I didn't think I could...not now. I mean, with my face all scratched and everything, I'd stand no chance at winning.'

'Is winning so important to you?'

'Yes,' she said vehemently. 'If I don't win, then I can't join the Lipstick Club.' At Jack's quizzical expression, she explained, 'It's a select club and you can only join once you've won a beauty contest.'

Jack nodded thoughtfully. 'This Lipstick Club must mean a lot to you.'

'It does.' She lowered her eyes to the magazine again. 'But now I'll never get in. Not looking like this.'

'Chantal.' Jack raised her chin so she was looking at him. 'You are a very attractive young lady. These bruises and cuts on your face are superficial. They'll be completely gone by the time the competition comes around. Trust me.'

'I want to,' she replied, 'but the other problem is that the entries close at the end of next week. I have to submit several photographs with the entry form and I'm not really photogenic at the moment.'

'No,' Mrs McBain agreed, 'but you had some taken only a few weeks ago. Can't we submit them instead?'

Chantal seemed to consider this proposal. 'The entry guidelines say they must be recent photographs... A few weeks ago could be considered recent.'

'And there were some lovely ones among them.'

A light of hope appeared in Chantal's eyes. 'Yes. Could you ask Dad to bring them in tonight?'

'We could have a family meeting and choose the best photographs together.' Mrs McBain's enthusiasm was contagious and soon Chantal was giggling with delight.

Jack's pager sounded and he rose from the bed. 'Unfortunately, I must go.'

'Will you come back again and visit?' Chantal asked eagerly. 'I'd like you to see the final selection of photographs—oh, you as well, Kathryn,' she added as an afterthought.

'I'd be honoured,' he replied. 'And now, if you ladies will excuse me, I'd better go and answer my page.' He gave Chantal and her mother his number one smile, before turning and giving Kathryn a wink.

'I'll go and ring your father now,' Mrs McBain said, and clapped her hands excitedly.

'In that case,' Kathryn said as she stepped forward and picked up Chantal's chart, 'let me have a quick look at your knee before I leave you with your plans.'

With Chantal's self-confidence returning by the second, Kathryn silently thanked Jack. The man was really quite extraordinary—especially where children were concerned.

Monday morning saw Steven a bundle of nerves as he began his intern orthopaedic rotation under Kathryn. His hand shook as he poured her a cup of coffee then sat down at the table in the kitchen.

'I don't want any special treatment,' Steven said. 'Just treat me like you would any other intern. Don't pick on me either. We're brother and sister at home but at the hospital we're consultant and intern.'

'Got it,' Kathryn replied, trying not to smile. 'I'm the big consultant and you're a lowly intern.'

'No. Don't be like that. So many consultants don't think us interns even have brains, and it's so insulting...' He broke off when Kathryn burst out laughing.

'I'm sorry, Steven. I know how difficult this must seem to you but relax, little brother. I try to be fair and respect everyone I work with, whether they're interns, registrars, enrolled nurses, registered nurses, cleaners or kitchen hands. We're all there to do important jobs and, as you've told me time and time again, the kids are the important ones. Just relax, Stevie.'

She stood and placed her hand on his shoulder. 'Thanks for the coffee but I think it's time we were getting to work. I expect my interns to be punctual,' she teased, and Steven groaned.

'The next two months are going to be endless.' He buried his head in his hand. 'Why, oh, why was I so overjoyed at the prospect of working with you?'

'Thanks for the vote of confidence.' Kathryn grinned.

'I didn't mean it like that. I meant... Oh, never mind. I'll see you there.'

Kathryn chuckled and left him sitting at the table as she went to her room to collect the work she'd done over the weekend. She had a task force report Jack needed first thing that morning.

'You just can't keep away from me, can you, Dr Pearce,' Jack teased as she handed him the report. 'How did Chantal respond to my attentions?'

Kathryn smiled. 'Like a duck to water.'

He ran his fingers through his hair. 'I have that effect on so many women. It's the natural Holden charm.'

'Whoa!' Kathryn said, ducking. 'I'd better get out of here quickly before your ego fills the room and suffocates me.' She headed for the door. 'I have to get to clinic or I'll end up running late all day.'

'Fine. Thanks for the report. We can discuss it further on Friday when you have dinner with me.'

Kathryn felt a stirring of anger at his tone but kept a rein on her temper. 'If you ask me, rather than tell me, Jack, I might just accept.'

'All right.' He came around his desk and took her hand in his. 'Do I need to go on bended knee or can I remain standing?' He tried hard not to laugh.

'You can stand,' she replied, feeling her temper subside.

'Will you do me the honour of...?' He hesitated and grinned wickedly at her, before continuing. 'Of having dinner with me on Friday night. Your choice of restaurant,' he added, as though to persuade her.

'Italian,' she said, and jerked her hand out of his. 'I'll pick you up at eight.' She walked to the door. 'And, Jack—be ready. I don't like to be kept waiting.'

She closed the door on his roar of laughter and grinned at his secretary.

Thankfully, Kathryn's clinic wasn't nearly as heavy as it usually was and she was able to slip out an hour before it was due to finish. Jack had taken Joel to Theatre at ten-thirty and it was now nearly eleven o'clock. She'd only missed the first half-hour and most of that was preparation.

She quickly changed and gowned, before slipping into the theatre. Hoping her presence would go unnoticed by Jack, as she hadn't asked his permission to watch, she was thwarted when the theatre sister said quite loudly, 'Why, Dr Pearce? What are you doing in here?'

'She's come to watch,' Jack replied, not taking his eyes from his small patient. There were a few gasps at the professor, breaking one of his rules. 'Come a little closer, Kathryn. I'm just about to make the initial incision.'

Kathryn did as he asked, being extremely careful not to come into contact with anything sterile. The scans were hooked onto the illuminated viewer so Jack could easily see where he had to go. The back of Joel's skull had been shaved, disinfected and draped. The anaesthetist was monitoring the patient very closely.

'Let's all offer up a silent prayer,' Jack said softly.

CHAPTER SEVEN

JACK made a vertical incision down the back of Joel's scalp and set to work to remove a section of the skull. Kathryn was intrigued and took a step sideways to get a better view. She looked at the firm muscles across Jack's back and had to decide momentarily whether she wanted to watch him or the operation. She smiled beneath her mask as she watched him work.

An hour later Jack said softly, 'Amazing!' She stood on tiptoe to get a better look. 'The tumour is completely encapsulated. It hasn't spread at all! This means we can excise it quite easily.' With the help of his assistants, Jack was able to remove the tumour, ordering it to be rushed off for pathology.

When Jack was ready to close he stapled the removed portion of the skull and then stapled the scalp closed. He took his time, making sure the job was done thoroughly. He turned and looked at Kathryn, giving her a wink. Although she couldn't see his mouth, the twinkle in his eyes told her he was smiling.

'Can you believe that?' he asked. 'Completely encapsulated! That's one fortunate little boy.'

Kathryn felt the tears begin to well in her eyes and nodded her agreement as Jack turned back to tend his patient. Slowly she made her way to the change rooms and reflected on the miracle that had just happened.

Once she was changed she went to Recovery to see Joel. His head was bandaged, his arm was bandaged and he had that awful-looking fixator on his leg—but he was alive. Time would heal his wounds and then he could live a normal life.

'Incredible, isn't it?' Jack said from behind her, and Kathryn turned, matching his radiant smile. 'This news is too good to tell Abigail over the phone. I'm going over to Adelaide General Hospital now to tell her face to face. Want to come?'

'I'd love to, Jack, but my own operating list starts in half an hour and I'd better get ready. Please pass on my regards and tell her how happy I am.' They both stood for a moment, watching their patient breathe in and out.

'I'm glad you were there to witness it.'

Belatedly, Kathryn realised she should apologise for not asking his permission to watch. She opened her mouth but he placed a hand on her shoulder.

'It's all right.' He grinned at her. 'I would have been surprised if you hadn't showed up. You're too good a doctor not to be concerned about your patient.'

'Thanks, Jack.' Their eyes held for a second before he removed his hand.

'Better be on my way. I can just imagine the worry Abigail and her husband have been going through. Time to cheer them up.' He gave her one last heart-warming smile, before walking out of Recovery.

Kathryn's week seemed to fly by at the speed of light. Prudence Florington's fracture improved faster, having her family—and especially her sister—with her twenty-four hours a day. Gregory generally stayed in the evenings, bringing his briefcase and office attire to the hospital so he could leave, after they'd all had breakfast, to go to work.

'Believe it or not, we have more time together in the mornings as the hospital is closer to Gregory's work. He doesn't have the half-hour drive to get to the office so we can relax with the girls,' Sally told Kathryn. The two women had become quite good friends and whenever Kathryn had a spare moment she would drop by to see her. On Wednesday they'd even managed to have lunch together in the cafeteria. The whole family was making the best out of a bad situation—something of which Kathryn wholeheartedly approved.

Earlier that morning she'd organised Chantal McBain's transfer to the rehabilitation hospital where she would undergo extensive physiotherapy to help restore the anterior and posterior cruciate ligaments.

'All set to go?' she'd asked as Chantal was lifted to an ambulance stretcher.

'Uh-huh,' the girl replied. Her mother was standing beside

the stretcher with a suitcase and several bags full of Chantal's belongings.

'You'd think she'd been here for a few months with the gear I've had to bring in,' Mrs McBain said with a smile.

'It's all been necessary, Mum,' Chantal reasoned. 'Besides, I had to look my best when Jack came around this morning.'

Kathryn smiled. Even though he was concerned with so many different patients of his own, Joel Brooks being top of the list at the moment, Jack had still found time to pop in and say goodbye to Chantal.

'Well, I'm glad you got to say goodbye,' Kathryn said. 'I'll be around in a few days to review your progress and then I'll be signing your treatment over to the specialists at the rehabilitation hospital.'

Chantal was too absorbed in studying her nail polish to hear, but Mrs McBain nodded in acknowledgment.

'Thank you for everything, Kathryn. You've done a marvellous job.'

'That's what I'm here for.' Kathryn smiled back, accepting the compliment. 'I'll be keeping in close contact with the specialists at the rehab hospital so you definitely haven't seen the last of me.'

'Good,' Mrs McBain said. The paramedics got Kathryn to sign Chantal's release form and wheeled her out of the ward. Even though it would take a while, Chantal was well on her way to recovery. Another satisfied customer.

Thursday was Kathryn's full day in Theatre, and just after lunch Jack tracked her down in the doctors' lounge.

'I presume you already know that Joel's tumour was benign?'

'Yes. I had heard.' She smiled at him.

'Kathryn, I need to ask a favour,' he said as he helped himself to coffee and sat opposite her. 'Emergency Theatres are busy and all other theatre time has been allocated. Have you got any room on your list this afternoon?'

'As a matter of fact, I have. I have about forty-five minutes spare because a knee arthroscopy's been cancelled.'

'Fantastic.'

'What's the problem?'

'Joel Brooks.'

Kathryn's heart sank at his words. 'What's wrong? I thought everything was going fine.'

'It was—until a few hours ago. There's fluid seeping through the staples. I've done a scan and the cerebrospinal fluid isn't draining properly. The pressure bandage that's been on his head since his initial surgery on Monday hasn't worked. I need to do a lumbar puncture and drain some fluid out to take pressure off the scalp.'

Kathryn gave a shudder.

'What's wrong?' Jack asked as a frown creased his forehead.

'It's the words "lumbar puncture". I've only done a few and even then it was under duress. Quite a few surgeons have their pet hates—mine is performing that task. I mean, you have to be pretty certain where you're passing that needle. The passage between the two vertebrae of the spine into the cerebrospinal fluid...' She gave another involuntary shudder.

Jack's eyebrows had gone from a frown to being raised. 'Well, well. The great Dr Pearce shows a small sign of weakness.'

Kathryn gave a dramatic sigh. 'Please don't tell anyone, but enough jokes. Poor Joel—my heart goes out to him. Have you spoken to his mother?'

'Yes.' He ran a hand through his hair and gave her a grin. 'I put her in a wheelchair yesterday and brought her over to see him. It was wonderful. Joel smiled for the first time since the accident. It's so hard on them all—to have this happen is like taking one step forwards and two steps backwards.'

'How successful do you think the lumbar puncture will be?'

'Hopefully, it will do the trick. If I put another pressure bandage around his head so the scalp doesn't swell it should fix itself.'

'But if you don't do the lumbar puncture you risk meningitis,' Kathryn reasoned.

'That's right, and the last thing Joel needs is meningitis. So, if you're agreeable, I'll slot him into your list. When will you be finished operating?'

Kathryn checked the clock. 'It's half past two now. I should be done by four.'

'Great.' He stood and took his cup to the sink. 'I'll get things organised.' Jack turned and smiled at her. 'You're welcome to assist, if you like.'

'Thank you *so much*, Professor,' she replied sweetly, knowing he was trying to wind her up, 'but I'll leave it to the experts.'

'As you wish.' He chuckled and went to get ready.

The next day was Friday, and Kathryn's morning clinic was so busy she didn't have time to ring Jack to find out how Joel had responded overnight to the lumbar puncture. In the afternoon she was standing outside the bank of lifts, waiting not so patiently for one to arrive, when he walked up behind her.

'If you took the stairs, you'd get there faster,' he said into her ear. Goosebumps cascaded down her arm and she turned to look at him. 'Or aren't you as fit as you thought you were?'

Kathryn grinned and pointed to the metal trolley beside her, which was full of different specimens in tightly sealed glass jars. 'I don't think I could carry these up the stairs,' she replied. 'How's Joel doing?'

'The fluid doesn't seem to be building up any more. He's being monitored closely so we'll see how it goes.'

Kathryn nodded at his explanation and smiled as he looked at the contents of her trolley.

'What are they for?' He eyed the murky depths of one jar.

'Teaching purposes. I think it's important for interns to use their initiative skills in diagnosing.'

'What *is* this?' Jack picked up a jar and turned it upside down. The gunk glopped downwards and Kathryn giggled.

'It's mud. Now you know what I do with my spare time. I make mud pies.' She leaned forward and pressed the button for the lift—again.

Jack replaced the jar and smiled at her. 'You do realise, Kathryn, it doesn't matter how many times you press the button it won't bring the lift here any faster.'

'I know. But it certainly helps to relieve frustration. I've been waiting here for almost ten minutes.' She sighed and planted her hands on her hips. 'I guess it's good to know that hospitals all over the country have slow lifts. Do you think they purposely get quotes from lift builders to see which one goes the slowest?'

'Calm down,' he said with a chuckle. 'And they're not called lift builders, they're called—'

'I don't really care, Jack. I just want to get these specimens to the teaching lab, three floors up, before lunchtime.'

'You're so impatient,' he said, and she thanked him for the compliment. 'However do you cope in Theatre?'

'Theatre's different. There's no room for impatience as it usually causes errors.' She pressed the up button again then the down button to see if that got any response. Soon after that the little light between them flashed up the message, 'Out of Order'.

'What?' She threw her hands in the air.

'You've done it now, Kathryn. You've pressed those buttons too many times and broken it.'

'I did not,' she told him. 'Great. Well, it looks as though I'll just have to lug these things up a few at a time. Although if I'd done that in the first place, instead of waiting here for the lift, then I'd probably be finished by now.'

'Probably,' Jack conceded as he gathered three jars off the trolley. 'What do you have in here? Bricks?'

'No. Brick powder is in that one over there.' She pointed to another jar.

'Come on. We'll get it done faster if we stop talking and start climbing those stairs.'

'Are you sure you're fit enough?' Kathryn couldn't resist teasing him.

'Do you want me to help or not?' Jack asked, but didn't wait for an answer and preceded her to the stairs.

With the two of them doing it, they only had to make two trips. Once Kathryn had organised the room, she locked the door and turned to Jack.

'Thanks.'

'No problem.' He glanced at his watch. 'I'd better be going but I'll see you tonight. Eight o'clock and I'll be ready.'

'Dress casually,' she called to his retreating back, and then grinned to herself. She was looking forward to tonight.

Kathryn gave a sharp knock on his wooden door and waited for it to be opened. She was dressed in her best denim jeans and wore a woollen jumper over her shirt. Even though the season had officially turned from winter to spring, it was still quite cool tonight.

'Hi,' Jack said when he opened the door. His eyes gently caressed her body as he inspected her clothes. 'A bit different from last time,' he remarked. Jack had taken heed of her instructions of that morning and was dressed similarly in denims, with a long-sleeved white shirt covering his torso. Reaching for his black leather jacket, he closed the door behind him and waited for her to move.

'Black leather, huh?' She openly gaped as he slung the jacket on, stuck his thumbs in his jeans pocket and slouched.

'You like?' he asked in that deep, resonant voice she'd often dreamt about. The fact that her jaw was almost hanging to her knees was perhaps an understatement of a reply. Kathryn nodded and closed her mouth.

'You look...good.' She turned and headed toward her car.

'Good? That's it?' He straightened and followed her. 'We're going to have to work on your vocabulary, Katy.' He stood beside the small Mazda and gave a wry chuckle. 'You expect me to fit in *there*? I don't think so. We can take my car.'

'No,' she replied firmly. 'You'll *fit* just fine. It's my turn to take you out so do as you're told and get into the car.' She grinned at him and had immense pleasure in watching Jack fold himself into the car, his knees almost around his ears. Sliding into the seat, she took a deep breath and started the engine. She was still recovering from the fact that Jack had called her Katy.

Not that she minded. In fact, she rather liked the way the nickname rolled off his tongue, and she realised he'd done it unconsciously. She hoped it was a sign that he was beginning to trust her and, if that was the case, she couldn't help wondering if he was going to tell her about Jill.

Not only did she need to know what had happened in Africa all those years ago, but she desperately wanted to discover exactly what Jack's relationship had been with her sister. Had they been just good friends? Lovers? She shook her head to clear her thoughts and concentrated on the directions Steven had given her to the restaurant.

She negotiated the car into a small parking space. 'See, if we'd brought your Jag we'd have been driving around for hours, trying to get a parking space.'

Jack opened the door and rolled himself onto the pavement, before uncurling himself. 'Ah-h,' he breathed as he stretched and stood up. 'That's better.'

Kathryn laughed at his antics as they walked toward the restaurant. 'I've never eaten here before but Steven told me the food is wonderful.' They could hear the beat of a popular song, blaring from the speakers at either end of the restaurant. 'Apparently, a lot of uni students hang out here,' she said into his ear.

'Great,' he replied without enthusiasm. 'Are you sure you don't want to go somewhere else? Somewhere a bit...quieter?'

'Getting old, Jack?' she queried, and grinned at him as the young teenage waiter showed them to a table.

'Brings back memories, doesn't it?' Kathryn yelled. The music had come to an abrupt end and the last two words of her sentence carried across the now silent restaurant. A few people looked at them and smiled, before turning back to their food. Kathryn cringed but smiled good-naturedly. 'I hate it when that happens.'

Jack returned her smile and they were both thankful when the music began again, this time on a softer level. A large Italian man came over to their table, replacing their previous waiter.

'I'm Carlos and I own this place. I apologise for the music and have spoken to my son.' He angrily waved a hand in the direction of the bar where the teenage waiter was busy making coffees. 'Please allow me to recommend some specific dishes to you.' He continued with his spiel and after Kathryn and Jack had ordered he gave a small nod and left them alone.

'Why are we getting such special treatment?' she asked Jack.

'If you'd care to take a closer look, Kathryn, you'll realise we're the only ones here over the age of thirty,' Jack said with a wry grin.

Kathryn slowly looked around the room and realised he was

right. The fact that they weren't wearing jeans with holes in them, nor had their hair coloured or in dreadlocks, made them look a little conspicuous. 'I'll kill Steven,' she said between clenched teeth, and Jack laughed.

'I wouldn't go that far. After all, you've already pointed out what a good doctor he is. It would be a shame to have his career cut short. Let's forget your brother and simply enjoy the food. That's one area where most uni students and interns are correct. They know good food at a good price.'

Steven had been correct, Kathryn thought as she savoured every mouthful of her *tagliatelle puttanesca*. Jack had ordered a baked lasagne and pronounced it the best he'd ever eaten.

'Here.' He held a forkful to her lips. 'Try some.'

Kathryn swallowed and met his eyes. Tasting each other's food was extremely personal but she obediently opened her mouth to accept his offering. After her lips had closed around the food, Jack slowly withdrew the fork. It was heady stuff and Kathryn found the experience surprisingly seductive, as she had at the Japanese restaurant. She wanted to try it for herself.

'Here.' Her voice cracked and she cleared her throat. Twisting some tagliatelle onto the fork, she held it out to him. 'Try some of mine.' When he opened his mouth to accept the food his eyes acknowledged what she was trying to do, and Kathryn blushed.

'What's the matter?' he asked when he'd finished the mouthful.

Kathryn took a sip of her wine, before meeting his gaze. 'My parents share food. Old married couples share food. Teenagers in love share food. It displays...' She searched for the right word.

'Familiarity,' Jack supplied, and Kathryn nodded. 'I seem to recall feeding you sushi not so long ago. What's wrong with us tasting each other's food?'

'Well, we're not... What I mean is, we aren't...'

'Dating? Exclusive?' He gave her a devilish grin as he said, 'In love?'

If Kathryn had thought she was blushing before, it was nothing compared to now. 'Let's talk about something else.' She took another sip of her wine and concentrated on her meal.

Jack chuckled. 'If you insist.' The electrically charged atmosphere between them slowly dissipated to a comfortable, friendly level. After consuming mouth-watering desserts, Kathryn and Jack lingered over their coffee.

'This place brings back memories of a restaurant we used to hang out in when I went through uni.' Kathryn stirred her cappuccino. She had been waiting all evening for Jack to bring up the subject of her sister. Surely he was going to tell her what she wanted to know. Why else would he have been so eager to come? Then there had been the food-tasting but he hadn't said a word.

Kathryn, being her normal, impatient self, decided to take the bull by the horns and introduce the topic—in a roundabout kind of way.

'Do you remember the café across the road from the uni bar?' Jack nodded at her question. 'Did you eat there?'

'A few times but I don't remember the food was anything special.'

'It must have changed owners by the time I went through,' she said, and grinned at him.

'I'm only thirty-nine. I'm not *that* much older than you.'

'Seven years, Jack. Enough to make a difference where med school is concerned.' She tilted her head sideways and said thoughtfully, 'But you were the same year as Jill, weren't you? So you didn't go to med school directly?'

'That's right,' he replied cautiously. 'I travelled around the world for a few years, before settling down to my self-induced hard labour.'

Kathryn smiled sweetly. She could see him erecting an emotional wall in front of her and wondered how to stop it. 'Do you remember Professor Hampton?'

Jack gave her a sharp look, before nodding. 'Yes. He was the anatomy professor.'

'That's him. Didn't he have a temper? I always did my anatomy work before any other subject to ensure I was never in his bad books.'

'Were you always such a goody two-shoes?' he asked with a forced smile.

'Only where he was concerned.' Kathryn took a sip of her coffee. The moment she'd mentioned Jill's name he'd begun to clam up. May as well jump in and get it over and done with, she thought. She quickly chose the right words in her mind before saying, 'Why don't you tell me about your days in Africa? What made you decide to go?'

He'd just raised the cup to his lips when she spoke. He eyed her over the rim, before replacing it on the table. He swallowed. 'What makes you think I want to talk about it?'

Kathryn's patience was beginning to wane. 'Come on, Jack. I'm only trying to get to know you better.'

'No, you're not.' He stood and pushed back his chair. 'I know what you're trying to do, Kathryn, and, as I've already told you before, I won't discuss Africa or Jill with you. It's over.'

The strong jut of his jaw, set firmly in place, was her final answer. Kathryn drained her cappuccino and went to pay the bill. When she was finished she noticed that Jack had walked outside and wondered if he'd caught a taxi home. She rushed out of the restaurant, catching her breath as the cold night air hit her.

She saw him standing by her car with his hands shoved into his jeans pockets. He looked sexy, silhouetted beneath the dim streetlight. 'I guess he wants to go,' she mumbled as she walked to her car. Each step she took felt as though she were going to an execution—her own.

Why had she pushed him? she thought, and received the answer immediately—because she had a right to know. Jack obviously didn't trust her enough to tell her the real truth about Africa. The government had said everyone had been murdered. How had Jack Holden escaped? That was one of the thoughts which had plagued her since her discovery a few weeks ago.

When she reached the car she unlocked the doors and climbed behind the wheel. She didn't laugh when he squashed himself into the passenger seat. She didn't bat an eyelid when he said he wanted to be taken home. She did, however, get completely frustrated and irrational when he refused to talk to her—about anything.

'I don't understand why you won't tell me, Jack. You obviously don't trust me enough. Jill was my sister. I loved her so much. Do you know how hard it is to achieve closure when all you get is a letter from the government with a brief description of what happened? Let me tell you—you don't achieve closure. We had no funeral, no explanation, no nothing. You are the one person who can help me. Help my whole family. My mother took it the hardest. First she lost her husband and then she lost the only daughter from that marriage.

'With a few words, you have the ability to help four people come to terms with their decade-old grief. But you won't. You're too selfish to think about helping other people with their emotional problems.'

His head snapped around and Kathryn was silenced by the murderous gleam in his eye. He turned away from her, as though he could no longer stand to look in her direction, and this hurt Kathryn more.

When she pulled up outside his town house he didn't say a word. He unwound himself from the seat, before slamming the door and striding into his yard. Kathryn leaned her head against the steering-wheel and sobbed.

After a few minutes she put the car into gear and drove the few blocks back to her home. She'd blown it this time. She'd pushed him over the edge and there was now no hope of ever finding out about her sister—or discovering why Jack was so reluctant to talk about the only woman he'd ever loved.

'Hey, sis, you look like death warmed up,' Steven said the following morning when he entered the kitchen. 'Something you want to talk about?'

'Not really,' Kathryn replied as she sipped her coffee, her fingers clenched around the mug to warm her hands.

'Fair enough.' Steven shrugged and poured himself a cup. Kathryn could feel Steven watching her and in the end she turned from staring into space to look at him. She'd hardly slept a wink last night and knew her brother's description of her was spot-on.

'What do you want, Steven?'

'I think I'd like to cheer you up.' He sprang to his feet and adopted a Cupid pose. 'How about a round of archery this morning? You could imagine the bullseye is anyone you feel like and shoot them right between the eyes.'

His idea had potential, she thought as she took another sip of her coffee.

'It's also to celebrate the end of our first week of working together. Not bad, eh?'

It was impossible *not* to pay attention to him and she smiled. 'I don't know what you were expecting...'

'Only that my lovely and talented sister might turn into a monster. I should have known better.'

'Yes, you should have,' she agreed, and carried her mug to the sink. 'A complete round of archery?'

'That's right.'

'Good. I need a boost to my ego and you just volunteered to be the sacrificial lamb. Give me twenty minutes to shower and get ready.'

'You take for ever!' He threw his hands in the air but grinned at his sister.

'You'll wait for ever if that's your attitude. Remember, Stevie, you've only got through the first week with me. You've still got another seven to go.' She did a Vincent Price laugh as she walked out of the kitchen.

True to her word, Kathryn was ready twenty minutes later. Her fingers were almost itching to get to those targets, and she knew exactly whose image she would imagine on the bullseye.

They opted for Kathryn's car as Steven's was temporarily off the road. 'It's blown a head gasket.'

'What was wrong with it *last* week?'

'The radiator.' He grinned impishly.

'Why don't you buy a decent car?'

He shook his head in disgust at her question. 'Success has really gone to your head, hasn't it? Don't you remember exactly how much interns get paid? I can't afford a decent car. The patch-up jobs on my old bomb can be done in my spare time, but I don't have much of that either.'

Kathryn laughed. 'Poor little Stevie. All will turn out well in the end. Trust big sister Katy.'

He joined in her laughter and kept up a steady banter of his car's ailments until she pulled into the car park.

'I'll get my stuff from my locker in the female rest rooms while you hire some equipment,' she told him. She was still smirking from Steven's stories and was grateful to her younger brother. Where would she be without him?

When they walked out to the range Kathryn looked around idly for Jack. She dreaded bumping into him but reflected that he was probably at the hospital and, besides, it was a free country and she could go wherever she chose with whomever she chose.

'It's been quite a few months since I came out here and even then I brought a date who'd never shot before.' Steven rolled his eyes heavenward. 'Believe me, I never saw her again. She was dangerous.'

'Danger Will Robinson,' Kathryn said, mimicking the *Lost In Space* robot they'd watched for so many years. Steven cracked up laughing and tossed an arm about her shoulders.

'You're the greatest, Kath. I can always count on you to make me laugh.'

'I didn't know you needed to,' she replied, and returned his hug. She'd obviously been too absorbed in her own problems to notice Steven's behaviour. 'Come on, let's get the game under way so I can beat you.'

'Big words for a little girl,' he joked, and took his stance at the first target.

They chatted about different things as they made their way around. 'So what's troubling you?' Kathryn asked as they walked between targets.

'It took you long enough to realise I had a problem. I had to all but spell it out for you,' Steven chided good-naturedly.

'I don't know why you don't come right out and tell me. Why do you always wait until I ask?'

'Because you always have so much on your mind. Especially since you arrived here. I know your job is very demanding and your determination to succeed is paramount but I hate to bother you.'

Kathryn stopped walking and looked up at her brother. 'Let's get one thing straight. You are no bother. I always have time for you. I love you, Stevie. You're the only brother I've got and I want you to grab me by the scruff of the neck and say, ''Hey, sis. I need to talk.'' I promise, I'll always listen.'

'Well, you're not doing a good job, now,' Steven pointed out with a smile as he began to walk again. 'It's woman trouble.'

'And?' she prompted when he didn't say anything else.

'She's a vascular registrar.'

'Ah.' Realisation dawned, and Kathryn said, 'A vascular registrar who invited you to the pub early one morning?'

'That's the one. We're good friends and, well, she makes more money than I do. She can afford to eat at better restaurants. She drives a great car and has more time off than I do, but I'm crazy about her.'

'Have you asked her out?'

'No. Well, yes. Only as friends and generally in a group. But we talk and talk for ages and have so much in common.'

'If she likes you, Steven, she won't care about money or cars or restaurants. She'll care about you, and if she's just in it for the material gain then she's not worth the time of day.'

'Thanks, Kath,' he said wryly. 'You've been such a big help.'

'Don't be sarcastic,' she joked. 'It ruins your looks. I don't know what you want me to say, Steven. Why don't you invite her around to the apartment one night and cook her a meal? You're a great cook and I can help you prepare for it, then make myself scarce.'

'Has merit.' He nodded. 'I'll think about it.' They reached the next target and he played his shot. From there on Steven got better, and Kathryn wished his problem hadn't been solved. She was still ahead by one hundred points, but if she lost her concentration he'd catch her for sure.

It was the last target and Kathryn took her position, concentrating hard. Imagining the centre of the bullseye to be Jack's eyes, she shot the arrow right in the centre. 'Gotcha,' she whispered and felt a sense of justice.

'Dr Pearce.' A deep voice called across the bush.

Jack! Kathryn spun around to see him walking toward her.

'Yep?' Steven answered. Kathryn watched as Jack came to a

halt and turned in her brother's direction. Steven was leaning against a tree, slightly out of Jack's vision, but after a few more steps the two men saw each other.

'Hey. Good to see you, Prof.' Steven walked over and shook Jack's hand.

'I think you can call me Jack,' he said, and smiled. 'Your sister has a good aim.'

'Sure has. She's just beaten me by one hundred. I couldn't catch her.'

'I've played a round with her before. I'll give you some hints.'

'What are you doing here?' Kathryn asked briskly as she walked between the two men, breaking up the male tête-à-tête. Her worst fears were confirmed. Jack was going to pretend last night hadn't happened. Why couldn't he understand that until she knew the truth about Jill there was no way they could go forward in any sort of relationship other than professional. At the moment the last thing she wanted was for Jack to become friends with Steven.

'Good morning, Kathryn. Get out of the wrong side of bed?'

'I wouldn't if I were you,' Steven warned. 'It's taken me the best part of three hours to get her out of a bad mood.'

'Steven.' The one word from Kathryn was like a bullet but Steven stubbornly ignored it.

'She's a redhead,' he reasoned, and Jack nodded. 'Her temper is so volatile.'

'You don't need to tell me,' Jack replied. 'I found out the hard way.'

Kathryn couldn't stand it any longer and, after collecting her arrows, stormed off ahead of them but made sure she was still within hearing distance.

'How about me?' Steven asked, begging for sympathy. 'It's not only Kath who's like this. My other sister was worse and Mum, well, let's just say you never cross her when she's in a temper.'

Jack chuckled. At the mention of Steven's 'other sister' Kathryn looked over her shoulder to gauge Jack's reaction. After all, every time *she* mentioned her sister Jack clammed up. Not this time. Jack merely raised his eyebrows, before grinning at her and turning his attention back to Steven.

'Dad and I used to escape to the garage when the three of them got going.' Steven chuckled.

'Ah, the garage,' Jack acknowledged. 'The last true bastion of testosterone.'

'Oh, for heaven's sake,' Kathryn spluttered, before running up the stairs to the club house and into the female rest rooms. She stowed her equipment in the locker then splashed some cool water onto her face.

How dared they both talk about her as though she wasn't there! Steven should know better than to wind her up but Jack had simply enjoyed the show. She held up her hands to her flushed face as she thought about the two men who were waiting for her.

Steven she could forgive. Anything for her little brother. She'd never been able to stay angry with him for long. But Jack. He'd toyed with her emotions too many times. Every time she saw him she was either up or down. Why was it never constant? Why couldn't he simply tell her what had happened so they could get on and have a normal relationship?

Is that what you want? She looked at herself critically in the mirror and realised the truth of the situation. How could she have been so careless? How could she possibly have fallen in love with Jack Holden?

CHAPTER EIGHT

WHEN Kathryn joined Steven and Jack at the table she wondered if they could see her new discovery in her face. She felt as though it was evident to everyone.

'Would you like to order?' the waiter said from behind her, and Kathryn jumped out of her chair. 'I'm sorry, ma'am. I didn't mean to startle you,' the waiter quickly apologised.

Steven put a hand out to his sister. 'You OK, Kath?'

'I'm fine,' she snapped, and then gave him an apologetic smile. 'I'll have a short black,' she told the waiter.

'Would you like something sweet?' Jack asked, and Kathryn tried to avoid looking at him. 'A piece of cake?'

'They have a delicious-looking poppy seed cake, Kath,' Steven said, hoping to tempt her.

'No—thank you.' She added the last two words belatedly and stared just past Steven's shoulder until the waiter left. Her brother and Jack were going out of their way to be nice. And so they should, she reasoned. They'd insulted her by talking about her as though she wasn't there—especially when both of them knew how much she hated it.

She decided that making them suffer a little seemed like good retribution, but when her eyes accidentally met Jack's and she saw the unspoken apology in them she melted. He was a handsome brute and now that she recognised her feelings as pure love Kathryn was ready to forgive him anything.

Steven kept the conversation light while they had their drinks. Kathryn could feel the coffee begin to relax her and she slowly felt the tension slip from her body. The men were talking about a violent movie just released. It was as though, by mutual consent, no one wanted to talk shop.

'Any plans for tonight?' Jack asked, and Kathryn's heart hammered wildly against her ribs. Then she realised he was talking to her brother.

116

'Only a date with some books.'

'No plans to go out on the town and stay up for an early morning drink?'

Steven had the grace to colour at Jack's reminder of his drunkenness. 'You don't need to worry about me doing anything that stupid again. My darling sister had a calm and concise discussion with me and I've decided the give up the drink. At least,' he said sheepishly, 'until I graduate. Then I'll really have something to celebrate.'

'Good for you,' Jack said, and nodded in approval. 'So you'll be hitting the books this evening?'

'Yeah. This orthopaedic rotation is pretty difficult. Do you know what she had us doing yesterday?' Steven's eyes twinkled as he met his sister's.

'Using your initiative to figure out what was in specimen jars?' Jack guessed.

'She told you, didn't she? We were all quite surprised when she explained what she wanted us to do. ''We're interns,'' one of the guys whispered to me. ''We don't have time to play how many jelly beans in the jar.'''

'''Give her a chance,'' I whispered back. Do you know, he got nearly every single one wrong. Boy was he mad with himself. You brought him down a peg or two, sis, and we're all grateful for that.'

'Glad I could be of service.' She smiled at her brother, feeling better.

Jack's mobile phone shrilled to life and he quickly unsnapped it from his belt. He mumbled a few words into the mouthpiece, before closing it up and hooking it back where it belonged.

'Problems?' Kathryn asked, and he nodded.

'Thanks for your company,' he said, but looked directly at her as he stood up. 'I'd better go.'

'We have to go as well,' Steven said, rising to his feet and tugging his sister with him. Jack signed for their drinks and they walked out to the parking lot. It was quite a busy morning and the car park was full. She noticed a car parked across hers—her own little Mazda parked in. The car was a black Jaguar convertible.

Kathryn stopped walking and put her hands on her hips. 'That's a bit childish, isn't it?' she asked Jack.

He did a double take, before eyeing her warily. 'There was nowhere else to park and, considering I knew you, I didn't think you'd mind being parked in.'

'Oh, sure.' Kathryn dug her keys out and walked over to her car. She knew she was overreacting but couldn't stop herself. Unlocking the door, she turned to give him a cool stare. 'Would you kindly move it?'

Jack gave her his most heart-warming smile and Kathryn could feel her resolve slipping. She turned away and climbed into the car. She heard her brother say goodbye before the Jaguar roared to life.

Steven didn't say a word until they were almost home. 'You know, Kath, Jack's not such a bad bloke. Why do you give him such a hard time?'

'Stay out of it, Steven.'

'But I thought you two were getting along. You've dated a few times and I thought it went well.'

'There are...' Kathryn searched for the right words and glanced briefly at Steven '...issues that need to be resolved before Jack and I can enjoy a normal, healthy relationship.'

'So, why don't you resolve them?'

'It's not me, Steven. It's him.'

'Oh.' He changed the subject and they talked about the family plans for Christmas. 'Mum and Dad get back from their tour of Europe at the end of November so I think you and I should drive across to Melbourne and surprise them.'

'Sounds feasible,' Kathryn said, but her mind was elsewhere. She was trying to figure out how to cope with loving Jack but hating him at the same time.

Forty-eight hours later Jack came bursting into her office and stood in front of her desk.

'I'll be taking Joel Brooks back to Theatre this afternoon for another lumbar puncture.'

'Why?' Kathryn twiddled her pen between her thumb and forefinger while she told her racing heart to calm down.

'The first one wasn't successful. The fluid is still building up where the tumour was, and isn't draining properly. I know you don't like lumbar punctures but would you like to be there? I don't want you to feel that I'm purposefully excluding you in any way.'

'I didn't think that at all.' Kathryn looked down at her clinic list. 'When were you going to do it?'

'In half an hour. He's been vomiting all night so I had him prepped immediately.'

'I didn't know,' she said, feeling guilty. It was nearly eight-thirty and although she'd done her own ward round she hadn't been over to the neurosurgical ward to see little Joel. It was difficult when all her patients weren't together, but it wasn't any excuse.

'That's why I'm here. The ward sister said you hadn't been round.'

'Are you criticising me?' she asked sharply, and he shook his head.

'Katy, Katy, Katy. I know you're busy and when I heard you hadn't reviewed him I thought I'd come and tell you myself. Don't go jumping to conclusions.'

Kathryn felt the tension drain out of her. Perhaps it was the way he'd used her nickname that helped. She gave him a small smile. 'Sorry.' She stood. 'I'd like to see him before he's prepped so I'll just duck around now.'

'I'll come with you,' Jack said, and held her office door open for her.

'It's not necessary,' Kathryn said.

'Don't argue, Kathryn.' He closed her door and they walked side by side to the ward.

When they walked into Joel's room he was trying to pull the bandage off his teddy's head. 'No,' he said. 'No.' He tugged again and the nurse standing beside him was trying to reassure him.

Jack and Kathryn crossed to his bedside. 'What's the matter, Joel?'

'No.' He finally succeeded in pulling the bandage off his

teddy's head and threw it onto the floor. The nurse sighed in frustration.

'We've put a bandage around his teddy's head so that teddy is the same as Joel, but he seems to think that if the bandage comes off teddy's head then it can come off his head as well.'

'It's all right, Joel.' Jack sat on the side of the bed so he was closer to Joel's height. 'Teddy's going to get better and then the bandage can stay off for ever but for now...' Jack picked up the bandage Joel had thrown onto the floor and rolled it into a neat ball. 'We'll get teddy a new bandage.'

'Do we have any different coloured bandages?' Kathryn asked. 'Perhaps that might make a difference.'

'I'll see what I can find,' the nurse replied.

Kathryn watched as Jack took Ruffles from his coat pocket and the puppet began tickling Joel to make him smile. It worked. Jack was wonderful with children. Why did he have to look so adorable, playing and caring for children? She focused her attention on Joel and moved closer to his bedside.

A few seconds later Ruffles was attempting to tickle her, which made Joel's smile broaden. Kathryn shook her finger and pretended to tell the puppet off but when he tickled her again Joel actually gave a laugh. It was music to their ears. This little boy had every right to bellyache and scream at all of the injections and needles they'd poked and prodded him with but his spirits were generally quite uplifted—which had a domino effect on everyone around him.

The orderlies walked in the door and Kathryn glanced at her watch. It was time for Joel to be taken around to Theatres. The smile was immediately wiped off his face and Kathryn choked back on a sob.

'Here's teddy, mate,' Kathryn said as Joel began to shrink beneath his bed covers. He clutched at his teddy as the orderlies got his bed ready to take out of the ward. It was a policy in this hospital to wheel the children out in their beds, rather than transfer them to a barouche and then transfer them again to the operating table.

This way, Joel would be anaesthetised in his own bed and transferred when he was asleep. The reverse would happen once

Jack had completed the procedure and he would wake up in his own bed.

'I'd better get going,' Jack said to Kathryn, and indicated that she should follow him out of the room. They said goodbye to Joel and walked into the corridor.

'It cuts me up,' he said in a low whisper. 'I wish I didn't have to put him through another general anaesthetic and another lumbar puncture, but it has to be done.'

'I guess he needs a general anaesthetic because he won't be able to stay absolutely still during the procedure, doesn't he?'

'Unfortunately, yes—but perhaps in some way it's better that he's asleep.' He raked a hand through his hair as they walked to the end of the ward.

Kathryn gave him a smile, feeling he needed some reassurance from her. 'Go to it, Professor Holden. I'll try my hardest to make it to Theatre in time. Hopefully, my own patients in the clinic will co-operate.'

'Good. I'll see you in Theatre, then.' He gave her a nod and turned in the direction of the theatre block. Kathryn watched him go, her heart aching for him to hold her again, for him to put his arms around her tenderly, before kissing her senseless.

She walked back to her office to find her phone ringing. Once she'd dealt with the caller she reviewed her clinic schedule. A bit of juggling was called for but she could do it.

Half an hour later she walked into Theatre. Jack turned to look at her and their eyes held for a split second before he looked away and concentrated on his patient.

'It's awful,' one of the sisters said in her ear. 'Every time they wheel Joel's bed down to Theatre the little fellow goes as stiff as a board. He's so scared. It would give us great pleasure not to put him through this, but it's necessary. Let's hope this one works.'

Kathryn nodded in agreement as she watched Jack carefully insert the needle between two vertebrae of the spine. He withdrew the fluid, then the needle. He was good, she thought as a shudder ripped through her. At least Joel had the best possible surgeon he could get.

A new pressure bandage was secured around Joel's head to

try and guide the cerebrospinal fluid to flow in the correct direction.

When the procedure was finished Kathryn quickly changed back into her navy skirt and white shirt, before going to clinic. What she'd really wanted to do was to tell Jack how wonderful he was. How caring and sensitive he was toward his small patient. How she wanted him to be caring and sensitive toward her. Whenever they were alone together Kathryn's thoughts turned automatically to Jill. What had happened? Why couldn't he trust her enough to tell her the truth?

The hectic pace of the clinic pushed these thoughts from her mind, and in the afternoon she had her own operating list to contend with. After the last case had been done and she'd filled in the operation notes, Kathryn headed toward the neurosurgical ward.

Jack was standing at the nurses' station, talking softly to his registrar. He looked up and saw her, and motioned her to join them.

'What's wrong?' She knew by the way his brow was furrowed and his jaw was clenched that everything was not right.

'Joel's vomiting already. The lumbar puncture didn't work. We'll have to put a shunt in. I've organised to take him back to Theatre as soon as possible.'

'Mind if I stay?' she asked, and he relaxed slightly at her question.

'Not at all. You're more than welcome.'

'Can I see him?'

'Sure. Abigail's been with him since late morning. I organised for an orderly to bring her over in a wheelchair when Joel returned from the lumbar puncture. I've spoken to her doctor at Adelaide General Hospital and he's agreed to let her stay the night. There's not a lot she can do physically but emotionally that little boy needs his mother.'

When Jack and Kathryn entered the room Joel was lying on his bed, clutching his teddy—who had a new blue bandage around his head. Abigail was stroking his hair and his eyes were closed. Kathryn's heart turned over at the sight.

'He's just gone off to sleep,' Abigail whispered, and they both nodded. Kathryn walked over and took a look at his leg. The external fixator pin sites had healed well and there was no inflammation to be seen. She had been going to order an X-ray of his arm to check the healing process but, considering everything else the little boy had been put through, she decided to wait. It wasn't urgent.

Abigail gazed at him—sleeping peacefully at last—before looking up at the doctors. Both of her arms were in below-elbow plaster casts and around her neck she had a brace. Her ribs were firmly bandaged beneath her clothes but her legs were working fine.

'Would you like some sling supports for your arms?' Kathryn whispered, giving Abigail a worried look.

'I have some, thank you. They've only been off for a short while, but when the casts start to get heavy again I'll put them back on.'

Kathryn nodded and gave her a smile. Abigail looked apologetically at Jack. 'Do you have time to go over the operation with me again?'

'Certainly. Let's go into a treatment room so Joel can get some sleep.' They walked out of the room quietly and across the hall. Jack spoke to one of the nursing sisters, letting her know that Joel was alone and needed to be watched.

Jack waited until Kathryn and Abigail were seated before saying, 'We'll be inserting a shunt to move the excess cerebrospinal fluid from Joel's head to his abdomen. We do this by inserting a valve between Joel's skull and scalp. From the top of the valve runs a catheter—a piece of tubing—into the cerebrospinal fluid reservoir.

'When the pressure in the reservoir builds up, the valve will open and the fluid will go through the tube. The tube goes down his neck, across his chest and into his abdomen.'

'Why is the fluid building up?' Abigail asked.

'The fluid is building up because blood clots that formed after the tumour removal operation are blocking the same pathway the tumour blocked. By doing the lumbar punctures—withdrawing some of the cerebrospinal fluid from his spine—and applying the pressure bandage, we had hoped to clear the pathway and release the blood clots to get the fluid flowing in the right direction. That didn't work, but we had to try.'

'So the shunt is the only answer?' Abigail bit her lip nervously.

'Yes. The shunt will effectively drain the build-up of fluid and deposit it into the abdomen, where it will be absorbed into the general flow of things. This still allows for the regular amount of fluid to circulate through the brain and spinal canal.'

Abigail slowly nodded. 'I presume the shunt goes under the skin?'

'Yes. The initial incision will be just near his right ear.'

'What happens when he grows? He's only two and, well, little boys have a tendency to grow.'

Jack smiled. 'They do, don't they? There will be a coil of tubing in his stomach so when he grows the tubing simply stretches with him, without pulling on the shunt valve. When Joel's about ten years old we may need to add more tubing, but we'll take an X-ray and judge that later.

'Having a shunt will allow Joel to lead a normal life and that means he'll be riding bikes, kicking footballs—you know—generally being a little boy. But you'll need to be aware of the signs and symptoms of a blocked shunt.'

At the sight of Abigail's pale face Kathryn reached out a hand. 'It's all right, Abigail. You don't have to watch him every second of the day, but you need to be aware of the problems that can arise.'

'That's right. If he should, let's say, fall off a chair—probably because he wasn't sitting properly even after you'd told him a dozen times to sit still.' Jack's words brought a smile to Abigail's lips and she nodded as though she'd already been in that situation.

'If he fell back and knocked his head then you need to monitor him. If he complains of a headache, has a temperature, starts vomiting or is pale and clammy, get him up to the hospital immediately. If you suspect the shunt is blocked it's best to get him to hospital within four hours.'

'In fact,' Kathryn inserted, 'even if he doesn't have those symptoms and you're worried, bring him in anyway.'

'Exactly,' Jack confirmed.

'But I don't want to be labelled a neurotic mother,' Abigail said with a wavery smile.

'I'd rather be labelled a neurotic mother,' Kathryn said, 'and show I care about my child than sit back and do nothing when he could need attention. Let me tell you, Abigail, no one here will label you as such. You love Joel and as a mother you're naturally concerned about him. Even if there is nothing wrong with him it will put *your* mind at ease and that counts for a lot.'

'I'll write everything down for you and give you my card,' Jack said. 'In the first few weeks after you get home you're bound to have endless questions. Contact my secretary and she'll know how to track me down.'

'Home.' Abigail sighed wistfully. 'It seems so long since I've been home.'

Jack's registrar knocked on the door and opened it. 'We're ready for him.'

'Right.' Jack stood and helped Abigail to her feet. 'I'll be out as soon as possible to tell you how it went. Try and rest while he's gone because he'll be needing his mummy when he wakes up. That's one service we can't provide—only you can.'

'Thanks,' she replied, tears spilling over onto her cheeks. 'May I come with him to Theatre? Just until he's anaesthetised?'

'Most certainly,' Jack said invitingly. He gave her a smile, before heading off to Theatre. Kathryn stayed with Joel and Abigail as the orderlies pushed his bed out of the ward.

On the way to Theatre Joel woke up. He didn't cry. He didn't whimper. He just lay as still as a statue, but the anxiety was evident in his eyes. Abigail held his hand tightly. Kathryn knew he was a brave little boy and she tenderly stroked his hair as he was anaesthetised. The orderly assisted Abigail back to the ward, leaving Kathryn to get changed—ready to watch the procedure.

The operation went according to plan and Jack was happy with the result. After he'd de-gowned he gave Kathryn a brilliant smile. 'I'll go tell Abigail the good news.'

Kathryn watched him go. They still needed to watch Joel over the next twenty-four hours to make sure his body didn't reject the shunt.

After changing back into her clothes for the third time that day, Kathryn stopped by her office to collect some paperwork. It was almost nine o'clock and she was hungry and tired. She tried to recall what leftovers were in her freezer and came up blank.

'Kathryn.' Jack stood in the doorway. 'How about getting a bite to eat?'

Kathryn looked him up and down, her eyes feasting on the sight of him. Dressed in a crumpled white shirt with navy trousers, with his tie missing, Jack looked tired but gorgeous.

She cleared her throat, before meeting his gaze. 'I don't know, Jack. Every time we're alone we end up arguing. I'm too tired and too hungry to argue.'

'Good,' he said, and pulled her out of the office. He closed and locked the door, before slinging an arm casually around her shoulders. 'Let's forget the hospital, forget the pressures of tomorrow and forget Jill.'

When Kathryn opened her mouth he quickly said, 'I don't mean it that way, Kathryn. I simply want to forget the outside world and just enjoy being with you. No passes—unless you really want them.' He raised his eyebrows for emphasis. 'But, other than that, I want to sit, eat and relax.'

'Sounds like a good prescription,' she agreed. 'How about we stop off at the Indian restaurant down the street, get some rice and curry and go back to my place and eat in the lounge room?'

'Good idea. I'll meet you at the curry place.' He gave her shoulders a quick squeeze, before walking off in the direction of his car.

Kathryn shook her head as she climbed into her Mazda. She hoped it would work—the fact they would be alone. Could she put aside their difference of opinion and enjoy the evening? Her burning need to know about Jill was driving a wedge between them, but for tonight she would pretend Jack was interested in her for who she was. Not because she reminded him of her sister.

Kathryn crunched into another poppadam and looked at Jack. He was lounging on the floor opposite her, the food spread between them.

'When did Tim's wife die?' she asked softly.

'Last night. Tim called through to my secretary this morning. With concentrating on Joel, I forgot to mention it.'

'Have you spoken to him?' She felt she knew Tim Conway, even though she'd never met the director of orthopaedics, whose position she was temporarily filling.

'Not yet. I thought I'd leave it until tomorrow. He's probably had thousands of calls and arrangements to make. She had breast cancer and it was too far gone by the time they discovered it. Her death was inevitable. That's why he took the time off.'

'Do you think he'll want to come back to work?' She met Jack's eyes and he shrugged.

'He may but you've signed a contract, Kathryn. Tim is entitled to six months off, and if he wants to come back to work it will break your contract.'

The last thing Kathryn wanted to do at the moment was leave Adelaide, especially with the situation regarding Jill unresolved. But, considering his wife had just died, she thought Tim Conway might prefer to immerse himself in the rigmarole of hospital life.

'After such a traumatic event such as this, I request my staff to pass a psychological exam before they can return to work,' Jack stated matter-of-factly. 'The last thing our little patients need is a stressed-out surgeon who makes irrational decisions because he's redirecting all his grief and frustrations into his work.'

Kathryn agreed. 'I guess we'll just have to take things as they come.' She glanced at all the leftover food. 'I think we ordered too much.'

'I'm sure Steven will enjoy the leftovers,' Jack said with a chuckle as he helped Kathryn to pack things away.

'I'm sure he will.'

'Where is he tonight?' Jack asked as they carried the food into the kitchen. Kathryn plugged in the kettle and sat down at the table.

'Out somewhere.' She shrugged. 'Probably at the library. If he's not coming home he generally leaves a note for me.'

'How's it going with you two working together?'

'Not a problem. He's one of my low-life dogsbodies and I'm his boss. It's the way it's been all of our lives.' She laughed. 'Seriously, though, we're fine. Steven was a bit worried in the beginning but he soon realised things would work out.'

'Good.' Jack watched as Kathryn tried unsuccessfully to smother a yawn, before saying, 'Don't worry about the coffee. Why don't you go to bed?'

Kathryn wasn't sure whether it was the relaxed atmosphere they'd shared over the past hour and a half or the fact that fatigue had finally caught up with her because she said, 'Are you propositioning me, Professor Holden?'

Jack grinned and shook his head. 'You're in no position for any hanky-panky.'

'So, why don't you put me into the position?'

'Besides,' he said, ignoring her comment and pulling her to her feet, 'you'd hate me in the morning.'

'Probably,' she conceded. She walked him to the door and accepted the most wonderful goodnight kiss. Jack slowly eased his mouth from hers and unhooked her hands from around his neck.

'Sleep,' he said, and gave her hand a little squeeze. 'See you tomorrow.'

As Kathryn watched Jack walk toward his car a loud scream pierced the air followed by the sound of a crash. The silence that followed was eerie. Jack spun to look at her, then took off in the direction from which the sounds had come—the house across the street.

Kathryn was hard on his heels as they ran up the dimly lit driveway. The back door to the house opened and a middle-aged woman came out. She was dressed in a tracksuit and had slippers on her feet. She glared at Jack and Kathryn in alarm before recognition dawned on her face as Kathryn smiled at her.

'Hello, Mrs Ruckman.'

'You heard it, too, then. I've just checked Kevin's bedroom

and he's not there.' She ran a hand through her short brown hair. Kathryn knew that Kevin was the Ruckmans' only child.

'Kevin.' Jack began calling as he walked further into the back yard. There were overgrown shrubs and large trees along the fence line, and because the moon was barely out tonight it was difficult to see.

'Do you have a torch?' Kathryn asked, and Mrs Ruckman nodded.

'I'll go and get it.'

Kathryn and Jack continued to search, the dark shadows making their task difficult.

'He's here,' Jack called, and Kathryn followed the direction of his voice. 'Watch your step, Kathryn. There's a ladder on the ground.'

'Pulse?' Kathryn knelt down beside him and felt gently for the young boy.

'Yes.'

'Where are you?' Mrs Ruckman called as she shone the torch around the yard.

'Over here,' Kathryn said, and was soon bathed in a beam of light.

She accepted the torch from Mrs Ruckman and shone it over Kevin's still body. 'His breathing's fine at the moment,' she told his mother, 'but he's unconscious.'

'Shouldn't we get him into the house?' Mrs Ruckman's unsteady voice asked.

'I'm just checking him out,' Jack said as he ran his hands expertly over Kevin's skull. He then had Kathryn shine the torch away from Kevin's face but still casting enough light so he could check the boy's pupils.

'They're dilating,' he told Kathryn softly. 'We need an ambulance because I want him at the hospital as soon as possible, Mrs Ruckman. Could you make the call for us, please? And would you mind bringing out a blanket to put over him?'

She was gone without another word and Kathryn gave Jack a dubious look. 'Bad?'

'I hope not. I won't know until I can have a proper look into those pupils and get some X-rays done. Check his left arm, Kathryn. It didn't feel right when I briefly checked it before.'

Kathryn did as she was asked and nodded. 'Feels like a clean fracture. No breaks in the skin.' She checked his other limbs, before pronouncing them fine.

They didn't leave his side until the ambulance arrived. Jack spoke with the paramedics, before accompanying Kevin on the ride to the hospital. Kathryn offered to drive Mrs Ruckman who had, on Kathryn's instructions, packed an overnight bag for herself and her son and locked up the house.

'His budgie is missing,' she told Kathryn on the way. 'He insisted that his window was slightly open when he went to sleep tonight. The bird—Ernie—was in the cage, but Kevin must have let him out.' She shook her head in exasperation.

'The bird went out the window and Kevin decided to find him.' Kathryn completed the story.

'Ernie must have gone up into the tree, Kevin got the ladder and...'

'And then we know what happened from there. He obviously crept very quietly out of the house and retrieved the ladder.'

Mrs Ruckman sighed. 'I've told him often enough that Ernie is his responsibility.'

'So he didn't want to bother you. Also, there was the fact that he'd get into trouble if you knew he'd been up playing with the bird.'

'I usually check on him when I go to bed, but tonight I was later than usual. There was a good movie on television and it didn't finish until ten-thirty. It was just after that I heard the crash.'

'Don't go blaming yourself for any of this,' Kathryn told her. 'You're a parent. You're not a mind-reader or a magician. How old is Kevin now?'

'He's eleven.' She sighed again. 'If only Jerry was here.'

'Is he interstate again?' Kathryn asked, knowing that Mr Ruckman's business often took him away.

'Yes. He's back tomorrow evening.'

Kathryn pulled into the doctors' car park and brought the Mazda to a halt in her allotted parking space. They both rushed into the casualty department, where Kathryn told Mrs Ruckman to sit in the waiting area and she'd get the latest news.

She was told by the sister that Jack had taken Kevin directly to Radiology. 'He said those pupils didn't look good and wanted to know what was going on inside the brain. By the time he arrived the right pupil was back to usual size but the left one is still enlarged.'

Kathryn told Mrs Ruckman where they were, before racing off to the radiology department.

'I've ordered X-rays of his left arm as well,' Jack told her when he spotted her. 'I'm just waiting for the final set of films to be developed but so far everything looks quite good.'

'Good?' Kathryn repeated, her eyes widening in astonishment.

'Yes. I'd like to see Mrs Ruckman as soon as I have these final films. Is she waiting in Casualty?'

'Yes.'

Jack looked away from the X-ray he was viewing and gazed at her. 'Is that all you can say, Kathryn? If so, this is my lucky night.'

'No!' she said firmly.

'Here are the films, Prof,' the radiologist said. 'I'll be doing the arm now, Kathryn. Do you want them brought straight out?'

'Yes, please,' she replied.

'See,' Jack said as Kathryn scanned the evidence before them. 'From the size of his left pupil, we should be seeing a very different story to this one.'

'Why don't you go and ask Mrs Ruckman a few questions while I wait for these films? I'll probably see you back in Casualty with Kevin.'

By the time all the radiographs had been taken and Kevin was wheeled back to Casualty, Jack had discovered from Mrs Ruckman that Kevin's left pupil was naturally large.

'She said they'd noticed it a few years ago and their local doctor said it was nothing to worry about,' he told her as they sat in the doctors' room. 'I'd like a very large note made in his case notes regarding this. I also think a medical alert tag is necessary. Little boys tend to play a lot of sport, and sport can often lead to head injuries. How's the arm?'

'Simple fracture of the radius. Plaster of Paris for six to eight weeks and he'll be back to his usual self.'

'Kevin Ruckman sounds like one very fortunate boy. What was he doing out in the back yard in his pyjamas, using a ladder to climb a tree?'

Kathryn told him about the budgie and he nodded with comprehension. 'Didn't want to tell Mum what had happened because he knew he'd get into trouble.'

'That's right.'

The night sister poked her head around the door. 'Kevin Ruckman's regained consciousness.'

'Thank you,' they both replied, and went to see him. He was looking rather dazed at waking up to find himself in hospital.

'What happened?' he asked Kathryn in a small voice after they'd introduced themselves.

'Don't you remember? You fell off the ladder.'

'I know you,' he told her, a smile lighting his freckled face. 'You're the doctor lady who lives across the street.'

'That's right.' Kathryn brushed a lock of brown hair from his forehead. 'Can you tell me what happened?'

His eyes looked from her to Jack and then back again. 'Will I get into trouble?'

They both smiled. 'I think it's a bit late for that, mate,' Jack said. 'We're all just happy you're OK.'

'Where's Mum?'

'She's out in the waiting room.'

'Is she angry?'

'I don't think so,' Kathryn answered. Kevin was obviously reluctant to talk about it so she decided to prompt him a little further to get him going. 'Where did you get the ladder from?'

'From the garage,' he answered automatically, then realised what he'd said and clamped his right hand over his mouth. He then realised he couldn't move his left arm.

'You've broken your arm and I've put plaster on to fix it.'

'Cool,' he said, and tried to look down at his arm. 'Wait till the boys at soccer see this tomorrow.'

'I'm afraid you won't be going to soccer tomorrow, Kevin,' Jack said. 'I'd like you to stay in hospital tonight and we'll see how you are in the morning.'

He digested this information then nodded.

'I think we can call your mum in now.'

'No, wait. Don't you want me to tell you what happened?' Kevin didn't seem too anxious to see his mother. He was convinced she'd be angry.

'If you're ready to tell us,' Kathryn said.

'I was playing with Ernie—that's my budgie.' His face fell in sadness. 'I should have been asleep but I couldn't so I decided to play quietly in my room. Well, the window was open and then Ernie flew out and I saw him land in the tree. So I sneaked outside and went into the garage to get the ladder. I knew if I tried to climb the tree it would shake and scare him away,' he explained matter-of-factly.

'I was so close. I could see him sitting on the branch and I called to him. He looked at me and I reached out my hand but...he was too far away. So I went up another step on the ladder and then it started to wobble. I remember falling and then—nothing.' He gave a wistful sigh. 'I wish I knew where Ernie was.'

'Thank you for telling us what happened. I'll go and get your mum now—she really wants to see you, Kevin.'

When Mrs Ruckman entered his cubicle tears began to pour down his face. 'I'm sorry, Mum,' he said. She gave him a hug and held him while he cried. When his sobs subsided he looked up at her with a tear-stained face and said, 'What about Ernie, Mum? What if we can't find him?'

'I'm sorry Ernie might be gone, dear, but we can buy you a new budgie, if you'd like. We'll talk about it later.' She turned to look at Jack and Kathryn. 'Thank you for everything.'

'That's all right. I'll let the orderlies know he's ready for transfer and we'll both be around to see you in the morning,' Kathryn said.

'You'll probably have quite a big headache for the next few days, Kevin,' Jack said, 'so the nurses on the ward will give you some medicine to help take away the pain.'

Kevin nodded, then Jack and Kathryn left the boy and his mother alone.

'Can I offer you a ride back to my house?' Kathryn asked as she smothered a yawn.

'What an invitation,' Jack said dryly as he slung his arm around her shoulder and walked her out of the hospital. 'If you hadn't yawned I might have misinterpreted it.'

'I know,' she replied, and grinned at him. She drove them back to her place, garaged her car and then walked Jack to his.

'Now, where were we?' he asked as he drew her into his arms. 'That's right. I had given you a passionate goodnight kiss and told you to go to bed.'

'Alone,' she reminded him.

'Unfortunate, but true.' He bent his head and kissed her again. 'Sleep,' he said, and put her reluctantly from him.

'Sleep,' she said, smiling at him before he got into his car and drove off.

The next day both Jack and Kathryn reviewed Kevin Ruckman and pronounced him fit enough to return home.

'No school for two weeks, due to that concussion.'

'Yippee,' he said.

'No sport, no television, no music and not too much light,' Jack finished. Kevin's face fell. 'Then I'll see you in my clinic to find out how you're progressing. I believe Kathryn doesn't want to see you again for another six to eight weeks so you'll have plenty of time for your friends to sign your cast.'

Kevin smiled, before saying goodbye. A taxi had been ordered for the drive back to their house, and Kathryn told Mrs Ruckman to pop across and see either her or Steven if she had any further problems.

Afterwards, she visited Joel Brooks and was pleased to find him responding well to the shunt. A week later he was doing things he'd never done before.

'He's talking a lot more than usual,' a delighted Abigail told Jack and Kathryn when they reviewed him. 'My husband is improving and will be able to come and see Joel this afternoon. He's drawn a special picture for his daddy,' she said excitedly, and Kathryn smiled. 'Things are looking up—at last,' Abigail sighed. 'It's wonderful. Thank you—both—so much.'

'Glad we could help.' Jack grinned. When a sick patient began to get better the whole ward celebrated with them.

Two days later Kathryn walked into Prudence Florington's room and was astounded at the transformation. Her leg was still secure in the walking splint which ensured it would be kept straight for the next two weeks.

'I've told her we're going home but I think she's forgotten what home is.' Sally smiled down at her daughters. Penelope was running around the room while Prudence was glad to be sitting on a chair out of the hospital bed. 'Is she going to be able to walk with the splint on? She doesn't seem to want to get down and walk.'

'That's a common reaction. Remember the poor little darling has been lying in a bed for well over a month. Is it any wonder her legs need a refresher course on how to walk again? She'll be moving around within twenty-four hours after you get home, especially with all her own possessions around her again. Then you'll have to watch her like a hawk to make sure she doesn't undo the Velcro straps on the splint and try to take it off.'

'Oh, dear,' Sally groaned, but smiled at Kathryn. 'Between the two of them, I'm going to have my hands full more than usual. No offence, Kathryn, but we're all glad to be going home.'

'No offence taken. Although we may be saddened to see our patients go, we're all very happy when they make a good recovery—which Prudence has. You'll be back here in a few weeks so I can review her in my clinic, but if you have any questions or problems you call me. Promise?'

'Promise.' Sally nodded. 'I also hope you'll be able to come around for dinner within the next month.'

'Should be possible,' Kathryn said. She lifted Prudence up onto the bed and tickled her for a minute, before giving her a final examination. She was almost finished when Jack walked in.

'Wuffles!' Penelope squealed excitedly. She raced over to

Jack and began pulling on his trouser leg. 'Where's Wuffles?' Jack bent down and told Penelope to check his pocket. Sure enough, there was the puppet. Prudence began to squirm, eager to see the puppet. Sally lifted her off the bed and put her back in the chair. Jack brought Ruffles over to where she sat and entertained the girls once again.

'He's so good with them. He's often stopped by to say hello,' Sally said quietly as the two women stood back and watched him.

'Really?' Kathryn didn't take her eyes off Jack. 'I didn't know. He's very thoughtful.'

Sally gave her a nudge and winked at her. 'Why don't you bring Jack along when you come over for dinner?'

'Sally!' Kathryn blushed and the other woman laughed. 'It's not like that. We're—'

'Oh, please,' Sally interrupted. 'Don't insult my intelligence. You're crazy about him. Admit it.'

'What good will that do?' Kathryn replied.

'Trouble in paradise? Never mind, it will work itself out.'

Kathryn didn't reply. Instead, she watched as Jack and Ruffles made two little girls happy. He'd make the most wonderful father, she thought, and could easily picture him with two little girls. Her girls. *Their* girls.

Kathryn uncurled herself from the sofa, where she'd been watching an old black and white movie, and went to answer the knock at the door. It was a cool Sunday afternoon and she knew she should be outside, enjoying the brisk weather, but she didn't have the energy.

'Jack!' Her surprise was evident in her face and voice. It was evident that he was the last person she'd been expecting to see. 'Is anything wrong?'

'Yes. Why aren't you dressed?' He walked past her into the hall.

'Dressed for what?' She looked down at her tracksuit and decided it was perfect for watching TV.

'Our lunch date. I thought I told you.'

'No, you didn't,' she replied with a smile.

'How remiss of me,' he said, not sounding at all apologetic. 'Well, don't just sit there, Kathryn. Go and get changed.'

'But I—'

'Please,' he persisted. 'Do you want me to beg?'

She stood and looked at him, considering his last question.

'Forget it, because I won't. Wear something warm and leave your hair loose.' He flicked her usual braid. 'And if you're not out in ten minutes I'll be in to finish the job myself. In the meantime, I'll put the kettle on.'

When she stood there, with her arms folded across her chest, he said impatiently, 'Mush, woman.'

'I'm not a husky,' Kathryn said between clenched teeth but, nevertheless, went off to her room to change. He was so arrogant. Always expecting to get his own way. Well, the only reason she was now changing into something warm and brushing her hair loose was because she knew he would carry out his threat to do it all for her.

She eyed the large bed with the covers neatly arranged on top and knew that if Jack entered her room they'd be thrown haphazardly off the bed as he threw her down—his body would be the only covering she would need.

He would pull the warm black jumper over her head, holding her arms captive with one strong hand. The creamy satin of her skin would be revealed, her lacy black bra not covering much.

Slowly his head would lower and his mouth would open to trail warm kisses in the valley between her breasts. Kathryn could hear herself gasping as he flicked the front catch on her bra, exposing her completely to his view. Closing her eyes in anticipated delight, she would wait for him to draw the rosy peak into his mouth and bring that liquid fire to burn through her body.

'Kathryn.' He knocked briskly at her door and she turned back to the mirror. Raking the brush through her hair, she noticed her cheeks were full of colour and her eyes were wild with passionate excitement. Every night when she went to sleep she would dream about Jack, and now she was doing it in broad daylight.

'Kathryn,' he called again, and this time the door opened. He stood in the doorway and looked over her black jumper and skirt she'd pulled on. She tilted her head forward, her hair covering her face as she was unable to meet his gaze.

He crossed the floor and stood behind her. 'Ready to go?' he asked. When she didn't answer he gently placed his hands on her shoulders and turned her to face him. Tenderly he brushed the hair from her face and settled it over her shoulder. He lifted her chin so their eyes finally met.

At his intake of breath, Kathryn knew the dazed passion was still evident in her eyes. He glanced across at the bed and then back to her again, as though he, too, was having the same thoughts.

'Oh, honey,' he whispered, and gathered her close. She buried her head in his dark jacket and breathed in the scent of him. 'We have lousy timing.'

CHAPTER NINE

THEY spent a wonderful afternoon having lunch at a little country pub in the Barossa Valley, before touring some of the wineries. Neither drank much, happy just being together.

On the drive back to Adelaide they enjoyed a comfortable silence and Kathryn let her thoughts drift. imagining what it would be like to spend the rest of her life with this wonderful man. She knew Jack would make a terrific father and that their children would inherit his dazzling blue eyes. Steven would learn to relax around him and she knew instinctively her parents would welcome him with open arms.

Her next thought was about Jill. There was still so much unsaid between her and Jack, and Kathryn's fantasy disappeared from view. When would he be ready to talk? To trust her?

Kathryn's thoughts jumbled around in her head and she tried to put them into perspective. Every time she'd mentioned Jill and pressed Jack to tell her they'd argued and silently gone their separate ways to cool off.

Every time after that Kathryn had still been stewing at his reluctance to talk while Jack had appeared unshaken and totally in control. Kathryn had rationalised that his anger cooled more quickly than hers but now...

She thought back to the first meeting after their Japanese dinner when Jack had walked into Casualty. He'd knocked her senseless, dressed in a tuxedo. Her heart had pounded, her knees had weakened. The fact that he'd brought vampy Veronica with him had only heightened her anger, but when she'd cooled off it had made way for the more sensual feelings she felt for Jack.

After their second argument about Jill, Jack had openly flirted with her—in front of her brother—at the archery park. While she'd tried to hold on to her anger he'd mixed up her emotions and tied her in knots. So much so that she'd discovered she was in love with him.

Did he know she was in love with him? Had this all been part of his master plan? If he couldn't have Jill he'd have her younger sister, and the brute *knew* she was his for the taking. He'd ruthlessly manipulated her emotions and made her fall in love with him.

Kathryn's anger was bubbling under the surface when they finally arrived at her house.

He switched off the ignition and turned to face her. 'Are you free for a quiet dinner this evening?' When she didn't look at him, didn't reply, he glanced at his watch. 'It's almost six o'clock. We could order in an early meal, sit in the lounge room again and relax. Perhaps catch a movie on TV. What do you say?'

Oh, he was good, Kathryn thought, trying not to grind her teeth. He was very good at this seduction game. She took a deep breath and said calmly, 'I say no.' She turned to look at him and almost capitulated. She wouldn't allow him the satisfaction of realising she was angry with him. 'It's been a lovely after-noon, Jack, but I think I'd rather have an early night.'

His eyes lit up at the mention of her bed and Kathryn turned away. She reached for the doorhandle and climbed out of the car. 'Thanks. Goodnight.' She turned her back on him and walked to her front door. Once inside she leaned against it and listened as he revved the engine and drove away.

'Have you got a moment, Kathryn?' Kirstie, the clinic sister, asked as she put her head around Kathryn's consulting-room door. Kathryn said a few more words into the dictaphone and placed it on the table.

'What's the problem?' She rubbed her fingers against her temple and decided an emergency was the last thing she needed on a Monday morning.

It was less than twenty-four hours since Jack had dropped her home, and her nerves were still raw. She had looked through old photo albums of her family before and after Jill's death. She had laughed at some of the great memories they'd evoked, and cried at others.

The headache started shortly after she'd gone to bed.

Paracetamol hadn't helped and this morning the ache was still there. Niggling and persistent. She tried to focus her attention on what Kirstie was saying.

'A nine-year-old boy has just been brought into Casualty. Andy Harris has diagnosed a compound fracture to the right arm. He'd like you to check the patient to see if he can be booked onto your operating list for this afternoon.'

'Is he still in Cas?'

'Yes. Can I have him brought up?'

'Sure. Bring me the X-rays and notes before I see him, please.'

'Certainly,' Kirstie replied, and lingered a minute. 'Headache?' At Kathryn's nod she said, 'Would you like some paracetamol?'

'I took some earlier this morning. I think I might try another cup of coffee instead.'

'OK. I'll get this patient organised for you.'

Kathryn made herself some coffee and sipped it, feeling it warm her body. A compound fracture. Just what she didn't need. Not that it was a difficult operation, it was just another added complication in a day that seemed to be getting worse—and it was only just after nine a.m.

A compound fracture meant they couldn't manipulate the bone back into place and slap plaster on it. Instead, she'd have to fix it back together with plates and screws. After all, a compound fracture meant the skin was perforated at the fracture site and liable to become infected.

Kirstie came into the room and gave Kathryn the X-rays and notes. Draining her coffee-cup, she read the case notes and looked at the X-rays, before seeing nine-year-old Daniel Dickson.

The notes stated he'd been injured while fighting in the schoolyard this morning. Kathryn was a bit puzzled, considering the current time. School would only just be starting now. How had he managed to get into a fight so quickly? The X-rays confirmed the diagnosis of a compound fracture to the right ulna and radius.

The nurse showed Daniel and his mother through from the

waiting room to Kathryn's consulting room. He was quite tall for a nine-year-old and had a head of black hair. His body language was defensive, and if he'd been able to cross his arms in front of him, she was sure he would have. His teeth were clenched and his green eyes spoke of anger. His right arm was secured in a sling.

Kathryn stood behind her desk and held her hand out to his mother, who was dressed in a business suit. 'I'm Dr Kathryn Pearce.' She shook the woman's hand.

'Michelle Dickson,' the other woman replied curtly.

'Please have a seat.' She motioned to the two chairs on the opposite side of her desk.

'Aren't you going to examine me?' Daniel asked between clenched teeth.

'Not right away. First I'd like to ask a few more questions. You're not in any pain, I hope?' Kathryn quickly glanced down at the notes to double-check that Andy Harris had prescribed analgesics, which he had.

'No,' Daniel replied.

'Good. Why don't you start by telling me what happened?' She directed her question to Daniel, but his mother interceded.

'He was fighting in the schoolyard. He knows better than that and, as far as I'm concerned, his broken arm is his punishment for being so childish.'

Kathryn kept her expression neutral, her eyes concentrating on Daniel's wince of pain at his mother's words. It was as though she'd struck him.

'Mrs Dickson.' Kathryn stood again and indicated the door. 'Would you mind waiting outside for a few moments while I speak with Daniel alone?'

Mrs Dickson stood and exhaled on a breath. 'Just how long is all this going to take? I'm due back at the office for a brief in twenty minutes.'

'You're not going to leave me, are you?' Daniel turned worried eyes to his mother.

'I have work, Daniel. I can't waste time here at the hospital.' Her words were firm and efficient. 'You're more than capable of taking care of yourself but I now have to organise alternative care for the other children.'

'But, Mum...' Daniel pleaded with his mother as tears sprang into his eyes.

'If you could just wait outside for a few minutes, Mrs Dickson, we won't be long,' Kathryn said.

His mother collected the briefcase she'd placed on the floor beside the chair and left them alone. Daniel's anger was now directed at Kathryn. He slumped in his chair, being careful not to disturb the sling too much.

'Please tell me what happened this morning,' Kathryn said.

'But I've already *told* heaps of people what happened.'

'I don't specifically want to know why you were fighting or with whom,' Kathryn said. 'I would like to know everything that's happened to you since you woke up this morning.'

Daniel's mouth formed an O. 'Why? Is that gonna help you fix my arm?'

'No. Please, Daniel?' It hadn't taken her too long to figure out that there was an enormous underlying problem here, and unless it was brought out into the open Daniel would either break another arm or leg or worse—next time.

He glared at Kathryn for a few more moments and then said stiffly, 'I woke up, got my brother and my little sisters out of bed. Told them to get dressed and put their cereal out. I made our lunches and told them to pack their bags. I locked the house and we walked to the bus stop.'

He paused and gave her another angry look. Kathryn simply nodded, waiting for him to continue.

'Stuart Blackney was on the bus and he made fun of my sisters. I was real cool about it and told them to sit down and ignore him. I made them sit in the seat in front of me and my brother so they wouldn't hear what he was saying. He kept saying awful things about them, and when we got off the bus at school he started picking on me. Saying I was a sissy and a mummy's boy. I'd tried even harder to ignore him but then he pushed me. I fell down and my sisters started crying.' He pointed to his torn trousers.

'I grazed my knee but when I stood up he punched me in the

shoulder. He's two grades older than me but I'm not that much shorter than him. I punched him in the stomach and then he hit me again. I just kept punching him as hard as I could, even though I knew it was wrong. Then he pushed me again, much harder this time, and I lost my balance and fell down the steps leading to the classrooms.

'My arm hurt and hurt and for a while I couldn't move. My sisters were really crying now and so was my little brother. Some of the other kids came to see if I was all right. I heard someone tell Stuart Blackney that he'd killed me. Then Mr Cobb came over and carried me inside to the first-aid room.'

Kathryn was buzzing with questions but knew that if she interrupted Daniel might not continue. She gave him another nod. 'And then what?'

'Mr Cobb said my arm was broken and called the ambulance and my mum. Then the ambulance took me here and my mum was waiting when I arrived. Then I saw a nurse and then a doctor and then I had X-rays and then I had a needle and then I was told to come up here to see you and then you asked me to tell you everything that has happened this morning.'

He gave her a small smile when he'd finished, and Kathryn returned it. 'Thank you, Daniel. How old are your sisters and your brother?'

'Andrew's seven and Samantha and Patricia are six.'

'What time does your mum usually leave for the office?'

'Mum goes at six-thirty and dad goes at six.'

Kathryn hadn't been too sure whether Daniel's father was in the picture and was glad he'd mentioned it. 'What kind of work do they both do?'

'Mum's a really important lawyer and dad's an accountant. Dad's often out of town because he has lots of big customers in Sydney and Melbourne and...and other places.' Daniel was proud of his parents and their respective jobs, although there was still a lot of resentment in his body language.

'They sound like two very busy people,' Kathryn commented. 'So you look after your brother and sisters to help them out?'

'Yeah. Mum and Dad say because I'm the oldest that I have to. It's my responsibility.'

'Do you take care of them after school?'

He nodded. 'We used to go to after-school care but Mum and Dad were getting home too late so we now just go home and have something to eat and go to bed. Mum and Dad always come in and kiss us all goodnight when they get home but sometimes I'm too tired to remember.'

The poor kid, Kathryn thought. The responsibility his parents were putting on him was absolutely outrageous. She looked down at his arm and then back to his eyes. They weren't as hostile as they'd been previously, and she hoped that talking about things had made him feel a bit better inside. She'd have to call Clara Lexington, the social worker, and inform her of the situation.

Daniel couldn't go on like this. His mother had labelled him irresponsible and childish for fighting. And why shouldn't he be? He was only *nine* years old.

'OK. Why don't you sit up on the examination couch for me and I'll take a look at that arm?'

He did as she asked. 'Will I have to stay in hospital?'

'Yes, you will. To fix your arm I need to operate on it this afternoon. We'll put you to sleep and when you wake up it will all be fixed.'

'Will I have a plaster cast on?'

Kathryn shook her head. 'Sorry, Daniel, not this time around, but you will have a screw or two in your arm so don't go setting off any metal detectors.'

'Cool,' he said, as though having metal in your arm was the best thing he'd heard of.

'Did Andy Harris, the doctor you saw in Casualty, explain the operation to you and your mum?'

'Yeah, kind of. Mum understood but I got lost a few times.'

'That's understandable. Why don't you go and have a seat in the waiting room and ask your mum to come in. I'll see if she has any questions.'

She watched him get off the table. 'Thanks, Dr Pearce.'

He had very good manners. 'Call me Kathryn or Dr Kathryn if you prefer. That's what most of the other children here call me.' She could see him eyeing her lollypop jar. 'Unfortunately, you can't have a lolly just now, Daniel—in fact, you can't eat anything more until after your operation—but if you'd like to choose a lollypop now I'll make sure it's by your bed when you wake up. How does that sound?'

'How about *two* lollypops?' he bargained. 'Considering I'd have to wait.'

Kathryn smiled. 'OK. You can have two and it will be our little secret.'

He chose two and she put them into the pocket of her white coat. 'I'll see you very soon, but I'd better get your mother to sign the permission forms or we'll all be in big trouble.' She grinned at him and was thrilled to receive a big smile in return.

'I'll be there as soon as I can,' Michelle Dickson was saying into her mobile phone as she walked back into Kathryn's consulting room. She pressed a button to end the call and then stood in front of the desk. 'Where are the forms I need to sign?'

'Ah... Mrs Dickson, would you please sit down? I'd like to discuss some things with you.'

'I really don't have the time, Dr Pearce. I have to be in court in fifteen minutes and it will take me at least ten minutes to get there.' She thrust a business card at Kathryn. 'That's my husband's details, and my contact numbers have already been given to your staff.'

'But you don't understand...' Kathryn began.

'I understand completely. I know Daniel needs surgery on his arm and I understand the operation. Now, if I could sign those forms I'll be on my way.'

Kathryn took a deep breath. 'I'd like Daniel to see our social worker, Clara Lexington.'

That stopped Michelle Dickson dead in her tracks. 'Social worker? Whatever for? Because he was fighting?'

'No, Mrs Dickson, not because he was fighting but because of the massive responsibilities you and your husband place on a nine-year-old boy. He's practically raising his brother and sisters.'

'How dare you?' Michelle Dickson's voice cut through Kathryn like a knife.

'I dare because your son's health is at stake. He's well on the way to a mental breakdown and he's only nine years old.'

'Mental breakdown. You have no idea what you're talking about. Now let me sign the forms so I can get back to work.'

Kathryn pushed the forms to the edge of the desk and held out a pen. Michelle Dickson reached into her coat pocket and pulled out her own pen, blatantly ignoring the one Kathryn offered. She scribbled her signature on the required pages and, without looking at Kathryn, replaced her pen, clutched her briefcase and stalked out of the room.

Kathryn exhaled the breath she'd been holding. Poor Daniel. She reached for the phone and asked one of the nurses to organise Daniel's immediate admission. She paged Andy Harris and asked him make the arrangements for Daniel to be included as the final patient on her operating list for that afternoon. Then she contacted Clara Lexington and asked her to stop by as soon as possible so she could discuss the situation.

Your job is to operate on the patient and fix him up. Leave the emotional details to Clara, who's trained specifically for that task, she told herself, but knew the pep talk wouldn't make any difference.

Her head now throbbed uncontrollably and she struggled through the rest of her clinic with a pounding head and a heavy heart. The operating list took all of her concentration and when she'd finally finished Daniel's operation, manipulating the fracture back into position and fixing it with metal plates and screws before suturing the wound closed, she was completely washed out.

She hadn't accidentally bumped into Jack but knew that, regardless of what their personal problems were, she'd give anything to feel his comforting arms around her, understanding her dilemma regarding Daniel and soothing all her worries away with his tender loving care.

The next day Kathryn's headache wasn't as bad. She'd conned Steven into giving her shoulders a massage the night before, and it had made the world of difference.

She managed to catch up with Clara after the ward round that morning to discuss Daniel's case, and was pleased to hear the social worker had had a good discussion with Mr Dickson the night before.

'I agree with your initial assessment,' Clara told Kathryn as they sat in Kathryn's office. 'Hopefully something can be done to help Daniel out. I've offered the solution of the parents hiring a live-in housekeeper-cum-nanny, considering neither of them can cut back on the hours they work. I hope to speak with Mrs Dickson some time today but her secretary said her schedule is rather heavy.'

Kathryn shook her head. 'It makes me sad to think there are childless couples out there who would willingly give up their careers for a loving family of their own.'

'I know,' Clara replied, 'but Daniel's parents do love him and his siblings. They've just lost their focus and perhaps we can help them get it back. How is Daniel progressing medically this morning?'

'He was a little quiet when I did the ward round this morning but he did tell me that his father had organised a babysitter for the other kids and had actually spent some time with him last night.'

'Maybe this broken arm was a godsend as far as the Dickson family are concerned.'

'I hope you're right, Clara. It eases my load considerably, knowing that you truly care for these children and are able to help them. You do a great job.'

'Thanks, Kathryn.' Clara glanced at her watch. 'I'd better get going. I've got another appointment.'

'Yes, and I've got meetings. Thanks for the update and please keep me informed.'

'Will do.' Clara gave her a smile, before leaving her office. Kathryn gathered up the papers she needed and went on her way.

She avoided Jack after the weekly meeting and was congratulating herself on another lucky escape as she climbed into the lift to go back down to her office.

'Hold the door,' she heard a muffled voice call as the doors began to close. Kathryn hit the 'door open' button and then wished she hadn't bothered.

'Thank you,' Jack said as he stepped into the lift. He gave her a lopsided smile and punched the button of the floor he wanted. 'Are you avoiding me?'

'I...um,' Kathryn stammered as the lift came to a jolting halt. 'What was that?'

There was a deafening silence around them and she lunged for the button panel. She pressed anything and everything—nothing happened.

'I'd say we're stuck,' Jack drawled as he sat on the floor, placing his folder of papers beside him. 'Why don't you sit down and relax, Kathryn? Pressing the buttons isn't going to make one bit of difference. This lift's been playing up for quite some time.'

Kathryn eyed the space of floor he patted beside him. Too close for comfort. She pressed the red emergency button again—nothing. Not even a bell ringing. 'I thought these lifts were supposed to have emergency phones,' she said, looking around the four walls of the enclosed space.

'They generally do, but these lifts came over on the ark. There's nothing to do but wait it out. A repair crew will be here as soon as possible. In the meantime...' he patted the floor beside him again '...let's discuss the theatre task force problem.'

Kathryn knew he was right and reluctantly gave in. She lowered herself as gracefully as she could, berating herself for wearing her long, pencil-thin skirt today, then took great care in placing her own folder of papers on the floor. Anything to delay the inevitable.

'Isn't that better?' he asked, and raised that wicked eyebrow at her. Her heart hammered in her throat, a sensation she was slowly getting used to. All she could do was nod and keep her eyes averted from his hypnotic gaze.

'After we've established the correct protocols,' he said, reaching for her hand, 'we'll send it to the director of theatres for his approval.' Jack's thumb began to rub gently back and forth over Kathryn's wrist, causing havoc with her pulse. She was sure he could feel it but he continued to talk in the same businesslike tone.

Kathryn swallowed and licked her suddenly dry lips. 'What do we do after that?' There was no mistaking the tremor in her words. His caress was making her lose all rational thought. Theatre task force be damned. The warmth of his shoulder pressed against hers, her hand encased firmly in his. The scent of his aftershave, the memory of the taste of his lips. She closed her eyes and rested her head against the wall.

He was talking to her but his words were fuzzy and distant, not penetrating the haze of the sensuality he exuded.

'Kathryn.' The way he softly said her name made her open her eyes. He was kneeling in front of her, his head close to her own. 'Kathryn,' he repeated, and let go of her hand to cup her face.

'Oh, Jack,' she whispered as he brought his mouth down, hungrily devouring her own. She lifted her hands to his hair and plunged them in, holding his head in place. She put her heart and soul into the kiss. Letting him know without words just how much she loved him. Didn't he realise how much she needed him?

Jack urged her around and gently pushed her backwards so she was lying on the floor. Something was digging into her back and she quickly reached underneath her body and pushed her folder away. The contents flew across the floor.

His mouth never leaving hers, Jack eased himself on top of Kathryn and finally brought their bodies into contact. She groaned as he deepened the kiss, his tongue plundering the depths of her mouth. Seeking, tasting, knowing.

Kathryn ran her hands along his back, enjoying the sensations of his well-defined muscles beneath his cotton shirt. Feeling denied of touching the real thing, she gently tugged his shirt from the band of his trousers. Finally her fingers ran up and over his back, her nails delicately scratching the surface.

Jack groaned and lifted his head to look down at her. His eyes were smouldering with desire and Kathryn knew hers mirrored his emotion. How stupid of her to deny the attraction, the love between them.

The lift jolted, then lurched, and Kathryn momentarily clung to him. Then a bell started ringing in her head and she quickly shoved him off her. Springing to her feet, she heard something rip. She looked down at the back of her skirt and groaned, realising she'd torn the small split in the back even further so it now revealed more of her shapely legs.

Jack calmly stood, tucking in his shirt. 'Want some help with your papers?' He indicated the mess around the floor as the lift gave another sickening lurch. Kathryn automatically reached out for Jack, who dutifully held her close to him.

'Katy,' he breathed as he smiled down at her, 'we've got to stop meeting like this.'

The lift stopped its acrobatics and resumed its descent. She wriggled free of his hold and dropped to her knees to gather up the papers. The lift doors opened to an audience of patiently waiting people.

The two of them must have looked a sight. Kathryn was on her hands and knees while Jack stood like the king, his hands on his hips and a grin on his face. Wishing her hair was loose to cover up her now very embarrassed face, Kathryn continued to collect her papers.

Jack bent to help her and her eyes briefly met his. She scanned his face, then closed her eyes as her embarrassment increased. Shoving the papers back into the folder, she allowed Jack to help her up before she stalked back to her office.

Closing the door, she leant against it and breathed hard. She raised a shaking hand to her lips, then looked at her finger. Smeared. By nightfall no one in the hospital would have any doubts as to what had happened in that lift. Their relationship wasn't a secret, but being part of hospital gossip irritated her. Kathryn pulled herself together and tried to look on the bright side. She'd have to tell Jack that her Sensuous Sunset lipstick didn't really suit him.

Kathryn tidied herself and reapplied her lipstick, before going back to the ward to check on Daniel. During the ward round that morning, he'd obviously been overwhelmed by all the doctors, nurses and interns that traipsed from one bed to another, asking questions and prodding patients, and he'd been reluctant to reply to any of her questions.

His operation yesterday afternoon had proceeded without any complications so, medically speaking, he was well on the way to a complete recovery. However, Kathryn was worried about his mental health. Even her discussion with Clara earlier today hadn't alleviated her concerns.

'Hi,' Kirstie said, bringing Kathryn out of her thoughts.

'What are you doing in the ward?' Kathryn smiled.

'Just dropping off some papers. How's the headache?'

Kathryn stopped where she was and realised it had gone. The headache which had plagued her for over twenty-four hours had disappeared. 'All gone,' she told Kirstie, who gave her a wink.

'I'm not surprised. Professor Holden has such a wonderful bedside manner. If you get tired of him, Kathryn, point him my way.'

Kathryn's jaw almost dropped to the ground as Kirstie waved goodbye and left the ward. Hospital grapevines were obviously working faster nowadays. She pushed the thought from her mind and went to see Daniel. Why was every member of staff on the ward giving her curious little smiles? Wishing she could go and hide, Kathryn pulled herself together. You're a professional, she told herself. Act like one.

'Hi, Dr Kathryn,' Daniel said brightly as she walked over to his bed.

'Hi. How's the arm feeling?' She picked up his chart from the end of the bed and scanned it quickly. All observations were normal, which was good to know.

'A little sore, but the nurse gave me a tablet that took the pain away.'

At the morning ward round she'd ordered another set of X-rays to be taken, and she showed them to Daniel.

'See, this is your arm and this is where I've put the metal plate and the screws. They'll hold the bone in place so that it can mend.' She checked his wound site and pronounced herself very satisfied. 'So, how are you settling in?'

'Great. I've made lots of new friends.' He pointed to the other boys who shared the large room. 'And guess what?' he asked excitedly. 'My dad came to see me last night. Just him—all by himself. He didn't bring Andrew, Patricia and Samantha with him. It was great. We played in the toy room and he taught me a card trick. I didn't know my dad could do card tricks.'

'That's fantastic. Can you show it to me?' she asked, her heart lifting at his progress. He did the trick and the other boys came over to watch. When he produced the card Kathryn had chosen the boys were in awe.

'Do it to me, Daniel,' one of them begged, and Daniel obliged.

Kathryn saw Clara out of the corner of her eye and walked over to talk with her.

'He's looking very happy,' Clara said.

'He's doing a card trick his father taught him. A little bit of attention from his dad and he's walking on sunshine.'

'Aren't *you* walking on sunshine as well, Kathryn?' Clara asked quietly with a small smile.

Kathryn buried her head in her hands. 'I can't win. The hospital grapevine has certainly done its work, but I really don't want to talk about it.'

Clara nodded. 'Anything you say. How about we talk about Daniel?'

'Much better topic,' Kathryn agreed.

'When were you planning on discharging him?'

'He can go home soon. His arm is fine and I need to review him in my clinic in a few weeks, but apart from that he could go home this evening.'

'Is it possible to delay it for a few days?'

'Why?'

Clara took a deep breath. 'I completely trust your judgement, Kathryn, that he's medically fit—but he's not emotionally fit. His father took the time last night to see his son and we had a very good talk. I truly believe that he'll get someone in to take the responsibility off Daniel's shoulders, but it may not happen for some time.'

'You think if Daniel goes home immediately, and copes with the responsibility within twenty-four hours of having his arm operated on, his parents will change their minds.'

'Exactly. With Daniel out of the way, they've been forced to make other arrangements. If he stays here for a few more days the arrangements can be made permanent. Look at it this way. If he goes home immediately the risk of him having a breakdown increases. Beside the fact that his mother still appears to be in denial that there is even a problem to begin with.'

Both she and Clara knew the hospital's policy was to fix 'em up and ship 'em out as soon as possible, but in Daniel's case they needed to bend the rules ever so slightly.

'Medically, he's fine, but if he becomes distraught the bones will take longer to heal,' Kathryn said meaningfully, and Clara nodded. 'So I'll accept your professional advice, Ms Lexington, and keep Daniel in for further observation for at least the next few days. We can review his situation then.'

'Thanks, Kathryn.'

'I'll go and make a note on his chart right now.'

'Oh, and, Kathryn,' Clara said innocently, but gave her friend a gentle smile, 'my door is always open if you need to talk.'

'I'll remember that,' Kathryn replied, and turned her flushed face away from the social worker's close scrutiny.

She made the necessary changes to Daniel's notes and advised the nursing staff of his extended stay. Daniel was busy laughing with his new friends so Kathryn left them to it and went around to the neurosurgical ward to check on Joel's arm and fixator.

The X-rays which had been taken earlier that morning had shown both fractures to be healing rapidly. If it wasn't for the external fixator, he could go home, but considering that both his parents still needed help themselves it was probably just as well.

As she walked down the neurosurgical ward to Joel's room she noticed similar grins and speculative glances from the staff to those she'd received in the orthopaedic ward. She continued on to Joel's room, without meeting anyone else's eye.

The shunt had now been in for two weeks and Joel was responding exceedingly well to the treatment. Kathryn was so happy for the little boy who'd looked so awful when he'd initially been brought into Casualty.

'Professor—Jack,' Abigail corrected herself, 'has been so

wonderful. He really is brilliant with the children, isn't he? Joel always has a special smile for Dr Jack when he comes around, don't you, darling?'

'Wes,' he said, for 'yes'. He showed Kathryn the picture he was drawing especially for Dr Jack.

'Are you going to do one for Dr Kathryn?' Abigail asked.

'Wes,' was Joel's reply as he nodded.

'Thank you,' Kathryn said, and gave him a big smile. 'I'll put it on my fridge at home.'

'P'omise?' he asked and Kathryn made the cross-my-heart sign.

'Promise.' He beamed at her words and kept on drawing.

'He's a different boy,' Abigail said with tears in her eyes. 'I can't believe the miracle that's happened. It's just so wonderful.'

Kathryn asked after her husband and was pleased to hear that his recovery was rapidly progressing. After spending a few more minutes with them, she said goodbye and went to the cafeteria. She was helping herself to coffee when Joan cornered her and guided her to a nearby table.

'Sit. Now tell me everything.' Joan's grin was from ear to ear and Kathryn couldn't help laughing. It was a welcome release.

'Why don't you tell me what you've heard, and I'll tell you if it's true,' she countered, and sipped her coffee.

'Only that you and Jack were stuck in the lift and were caught making love when the technician fixed the wretched contraption.'

Kathryn forced herself to smile. If the technician had taken another ten minutes to fix that 'wretched contraption' they might have been caught doing just that. 'He kissed me, that's all.' She shrugged.

'That's all? The most eligible, handsome and desirable man kisses you and you simply say that's all?' Joan threw her arms up in exasperation, then gave Kathryn a narrow look as realisation dawned. 'How long has this been going on?'

'A few weeks. I'm surprised the grapevine hasn't picked it up before now.'

'Well, there has been the odd rumour or two but that's nothing compared to the two of you wearing the same shade of lipstick this morning.'

'Yes. It didn't do much for Jack's complexion. He's more of a Passion Pink person, don't you think?'

The two women were laughing when a deep voice asked, 'What's Passion Pink?'

All traces of laughter were wiped from their faces as the subject of their discussion pulled up a chair and sat down. 'Keep going, ladies. I'm sure I'll enjoy it.'

'So you've heard the rumours, then,' Joan said with a smile.

'Heard them?' he grinned. 'I started them, of course.'

Joan laughed but Kathryn was shocked. Surely he was joking—wasn't he?

'Relax, Katy, darling,' he oozed, with honey dripping all over the place, and she saw Joan mouth, 'Katy, darling' with raised eyebrows. 'The cat's out of the bag. Looks like we're officially an item.'

'Kathryn's just told me it's been going on for a few weeks,' Joan said sternly to Jack. He looked at Kathryn with surprise but didn't say anything. 'Why didn't either of you tell me? I don't have a big mouth and I thought I was your friend but no. Instead I have to hear some third-hand gossip from one of my junior nurses.'

Jack leaned over and patted her hand. 'Joan, you know you'll always be number one in my life. Kathryn's just a momentary diversion.'

Joan slapped at his hand. 'Be sensible. If you continue like this, Jack Holden, you'll scare her off. If you want my advice, the two of you should marry as soon as possible. I knew the moment she walked into your office and nearly fainted that she was the right woman for you.' She stood up and assumed her best matronly pose. 'If you don't heed my warning, you'll be all alone. Both of you. Now, if you'll excuse me, I have some rumours to set back on a straight course.' She walked out of the cafeteria, leaving them alone. Something Kathryn didn't want.

She drank her coffee, without looking at him. Joan's idea that they should marry hung in the air. Finally she gathered up the nerve to look at him, only to find him smiling.

'If you dare say, "So how about it?" I'll clobber you, Jack Holden.'

The grin was wiped from his face and she wondered briefly if it was all an act or whether there was a chance he might be serious. No. She shook her head. He wasn't serious about marriage, especially not to her. Everyone at this hospital might think things were all rosy and cosy between them, but they both knew the truth about her sister would always keep them apart until Jack decided to trust her.

'I'd better go.' She stood and so did he.

'I'll walk with you,' he announced, and escorted her out of the cafeteria. She could feel nearly everyone staring at them and felt sick. Well, she'd just have to get used to it. Jack Holden was big news in this hospital and she would be forever labelled alongside him.

'Kathryn, I wanted to apologise for everything that's happened today. I'd offer to take full responsibility but it's a bit too late for that. Unfortunately, you're stuck with me—a prospect I hope you won't find too distasteful.'

'Jack...' she said, but he pulled her into an out-of-the-way corner and silenced her with a light finger across her lips.

'Just for the record, I didn't start the rumour. You know how this place works, and the evidence was pretty damning.' He grinned and she couldn't help smiling back. 'As far as what Joan said, who and when either of us marry is none of her business or anyone else's. Just ride out the storm, Kathryn. At least with people talking about us, they've stopped talking about Tim Conway and his wife.'

'True,' Kathryn conceded.

'I'd better go,' he said, looking at his watch. 'I'm due in Theatre. See you tomorrow.'

But she didn't see him tomorrow—or the next day. In fact, over the next week they hardly had time to touch base. Kathryn kept recalling the old saying that absence makes the heart grow fonder, and realised its true meaning.

On Monday morning she had a meeting with Clara, who pronounced herself satisfied with Daniel's condition and the arrangements his parents had made to remove some of the responsibility from those small shoulders.

'It's been a week today since Daniel broke his arm,' she told Kathryn in the privacy of her office. 'Mr Dickson said that his wife has slowly come around although they've had numerous arguments about it, but the proof is in the live-in housekeeper-cum-nanny they've hired. She's a retired widow, who is not only willing to look after the children but will provide them with a grandmother figure as well.

'Daniel's siblings have taken very well to her and, considering she has no other family of her own, it appears to be a perfect match. The children are now having a more balanced diet than the frozen microwavable dinners that were previously left in the freezer, and Mrs Dickson is coming home to a spotless house.'

'I'm glad to hear it,' Kathryn replied. 'I only hope it lasts and that this "grandmother figure" isn't too good to be true.'

'I've met her and she seems like a wonderful woman. She was more than willing for Mr Dickson to have an investigator check her background, and everything she's told him is absolutely true. No criminal record, no convictions, just a lonely woman with a strong maternal instinct.'

'Well, Daniel is more than ready to go home and, in fact, was asking me about it yesterday when I did a ward round. I told him I'd be talking with you this morning and would let him know as soon as we'd made a decision. His arm has healed very nicely and I only need to see him in my clinic in a month's time so I, too, can monitor the family situation.'

'Great,' Clara said with a smile. 'For my part, I'm satisfied with his mental condition and am all for him returning to the fold.'

Kathryn stood. 'Shall we go tell him the news?'

'Certainly.'

Kathryn locked her office, and as the two women walked to the ward Clara asked, 'So how are things going with Jack Holden?'

Kathryn sighed and Clara laughed. 'That good, huh?'

'We've both been so busy this past week that the only contact we've had have been a few brief phone calls either between theatre cases or clinics. I guess it's the downside of us both being such busy people.'

'I'm sure you'll work things out,' Clara said with certainty as they walked into Daniel's room. He wasn't there. Neither were any of the other boys.

'They're all in the playroom,' one of the nurses informed them. Sure enough, there was Daniel, racing around—being careful of his arm—playing with the other boys.

'You'd think all of them were playing hooky when you see them like this.' Kathryn's heart warmed at the sight of children, laughing and having fun.

'It does them the world of good. Better than any treatments *we* prescribe,' Clara agreed.

'Yet they go downhill so quickly. Daniel,' she called, and he looked over to where they stood. With a few strides he was standing in front of them.

'Can I go home today?' The beam on his face was a complete contrast to the boy who had walked through her clinic door only one week ago.

'You sure can. Clara's going to contact your parents to let them know you can be collected whenever they're ready.'

'Yippee!' he said. 'When Dad was here last night he said he'd pick me up especially. I guess that means I have to wait until he finishes work tonight but I don't care. It'll give me more time to play with my new friends.'

'OK. Off you go, but watch that arm. When I see you in my clinic in a few weeks' time I want to see the wound healed and I'll check that you've been doing the exercises the physiotherapist has told you to do.'

'Yes, Dr Kathryn,' he said in an impatient tone, eager to return to his friends.

'Another job well done,' Clara said, and Kathryn nodded.

'I'd better write up his discharge notes and get around to clinic. If I start late I generally finish late, which means I start my operating list late...' She let the sentence hang and shrugged.

'With no lunch in between,' Clara tut-tutted. 'Glad I'm a social worker, not a doctor.'

Kathryn smiled. 'Really? I'm glad I'm a doctor, not a social worker.'

Kathryn's clinic was as busy as usual but, thanks to a cancellation, she was able to finish on time. She was thankful the speculative glances had stopped and people seemed to accept her and Jack as a couple, which, she thought as she walked back from clinic to her office, probably wasn't such a good idea. Both of them knew they had unfinished business, but for the time being it was put on the back burner.

After finally finishing her clinic on Wednesday afternoon, Kathryn sat down at her desk and began to catch up on her paperwork. Five minutes later there was a sharp rap at her door, and she put her pen down and looked up. Steven stuck his head around, came in and closed the door.

'Sorry to bother you, but we need your help.'

'What's the problem?'

'It's Professor Holden.'

'Steven, I don't have...' She gestured to her desk, which was overflowing with papers.

'Just listen, Kath,' he interrupted. 'He's been in a foul mood all day and he's just bitten *Joan's* head off.'

The seriousness of his words sank in. Jack had the utmost respect for Joan and would never do anything to hurt her.

'What makes you think *I* can make a difference?'

'Oh, come off it, Kath,' Steven replied impatiently.

'What if he snaps *my* head off?'

'It won't be the first time.' He held up his hand. 'Sorry. I know that was a cheap shot but, honestly, Kath, you're our only hope.'

Kathryn sighed. 'Have you any idea what's wrong?'

'He's had a problem with a patient all week. A little girl of four. Her name's Melissa Freedman and she's a gorgeous child with blonde hair and big blue eyes. A real heart-stealer.'

Kathryn shuffled about on her desk for a piece of paper and stood up. 'Lock up my office, will you? Oh, and, Steven, if I'm not back in half an hour send in the cavalry.'

'Thanks, sis.' He grinned and watched as his sister marched off to battle.

CHAPTER TEN

JACK'S secretary smiled and mouthed 'good luck' as Kathryn walked past. That meant Jack was *really* in a bad mood. She knocked at his door and strode in.

'Sorry to bother you, Jack. Could you sign this requisition for me, please?'

Jack's head shot up and he glared at her. She almost faltered at the murderous look in his eyes. 'Requisition for what?'

'A new arthroscope for the orthopaedic theatres. The one we have now is on its last legs, pardon the pun.' She grinned, hoping her little joke would make him smile. Instead, his frown deepened.

'You don't need me to sign that. You're head of department. You can order whatever you like.'

Kathryn knew this to be true but she continued, 'The hospital requisition department doesn't recognise me as having authority. They'll take Tim's signature or yours.'

'Then a letter should be written to instruct them to keep updated with the changes of this hospital.' His voice held a vicious thread to it and Kathryn knew she'd have to proceed with caution.

'I agree. In the meantime...' She held out the form to him. He snatched up a pen and scribbled his signature on the dotted line. 'Thank you.' She lingered over his shoulder for a moment and he looked up at her.

'Was that all? Or have the masses sent you to deal with the lion?'

Kathryn perched herself seductively on the corner of his desk. 'I've never thought of you as a lion, Jack. More a panther. All dark and brooding.'

'Cut the crap, Kathryn. What do you want?' He raised his voice and stood up.

Kathryn took a breath and said calmly, 'I came to see if you wanted to talk. After all, we are officially an item.' She threw his words from last week back at him. They didn't make any difference.

'I don't want to discuss it.' He started pacing and she knew she was making progress. It seemed to her there were a number of things Jack didn't want to discuss. She'd heard of men bottling up their problems and emotions but this was ridiculous!

'What happened with Melissa?' she asked quietly, and he spun on his heel to face her.

'What do you know about it?'

'Nothing, other than her name. Why don't you tell me?' She walked around to a chair and sat down. Watching him pace the room with his hands deep in his pockets, she knew his small patient was really troubling him.

'Tell me, Jack,' she urged. 'You need to talk, and if you won't talk to me I'll officially request you see a member of the psychiatric staff.'

'You wouldn't dare,' he growled. 'You want to know what happened—I'll tell you.' His voice was deathly quiet and Kathryn swallowed the lump in her throat. 'I almost killed a four-year-old girl.'

'Jack...' Kathryn wasn't sure if he was exaggerating or not.

'If you want to know what happened then don't interrupt.'

'OK.' She held up her hands in defence and waited for him to continue.

'I operated on her last week to remove a medulloblastoma.' He looked at Kathryn's blank face and said impatiently, 'A malignant tumour that usually occurs in the cerebellum. In Melissa's case, this was where it was.' At Kathryn's nod he continued. 'At least, I *thought* it was a medulloblastoma. I excised the tumour and sent it away for pathology. Every case I've come across so far—*every* case—has been malignant.' He kept on pacing.

'She was recovering well but developed the same problem as Joel with cerebrospinal fluid. I didn't want to put a shunt in because, with the tumour being malignant, the shunt would carry the cancer around to her other organs at a faster rate, thereby decreasing her time to live.'

He stopped where he was, tilted his head to one side and looked at Kathryn. 'She suffered a mild stroke and two hours later Pathology told me the tumour was benign. That means the tumour just happened to be in the exact region that medullo-blastomas grow. It was just a benign tumour in the wrong spot. I should have realised that.'

Kathryn bit her tongue on her gasp of surprise. Jack didn't require any emotion or reaction from her, merely to listen.

'I took her to Theatre this morning and put the shunt in. She's responding well and, with rehabilitation for the stroke, will only have a five per cent loss of body function.'

'That's good odds,' Kathryn said quietly, but he shook his head.

'I should have done more tests. I should have been more thorough.'

'Don't start doubting your judgement, Jack. Second-guessing will get you nowhere. From what you've said, you've done the right thing. The correct procedure. There is no way you could have realised that tumour was benign until you'd removed it.'

'But she had a stroke. If I'd put the shunt in straight away it wouldn't have happened. The stroke could have been far worse and she could have died.'

'She didn't.' Kathryn slowly walked over to him and placed her hand on his arm. 'If you'd put that shunt in and the tumour had been malignant, you would have sealed her fate. I'll bet *everyone*, including the pathology department, was as surprised as you that the tumour was benign.' She looked up at him with love in her eyes and said earnestly, 'But you didn't do anything wrong, Jack. In fact, you've given Melissa a great start. Every day is going to be a special day for her and her family.'

'It could have gone so wrong.' He shook his head.

'It didn't. You're not God. You couldn't foresee any of this, but when the situation arose you handled it correctly. How did her parents react to the news?'

'They're happy it's not malignant and they understand the reasons for the shunt not going in sooner.'

'See. How is Melissa progressing?'

'Better than expected.' He felt a weight lift from his shoulders and he looked down at Kathryn. A smile slowly touched his lips as his head descended. 'You are so perfect for me.'

Kathryn closed her eyes and threaded her fingers through his hair. Even though things weren't right between them, Jack had opened up to her. It was an enormous step for him to take and her love for him grew even more.

She pressed her body against his and he gathered her closer. The feel of his muscled torso and the heat radiating from him sent tingles down her spine.

'See how perfect you are for me,' he growled as he nibbled her earlobe. 'We fit perfectly. My body to your body.' He kissed her lips once more, before drawing away. 'Unfortunately, much as I'd love to continue our dalliance, I doubt my secretary would appreciate it if she were to walk in.'

'Why? She knows we're a couple—as does the rest of the hospital, for that matter,' Kathryn grumbled as he walked over to his desk.

'I know we're public knowledge but I don't want to add fuel to the fire by pushing everything off my desk and making love to you—right here, right now.'

Kathryn's eyes widened at his words and she walked over to him. She ran her hand over the desk-top.

'Bit cool but I guess you'd warm it up.'

'Don't tempt me,' he warned. 'It was difficult enough to walk away from you just now.' He took her hand in his and pulled her towards the door. 'I think we'd better get out of this room and somewhere public before we both lose control.'

'Where?'

'ICU.'

'Well that certainly douses the flames. Nothing like work to kill the romantic mood,' she said, and Jack chuckled.

'Not work, exactly. I'd like you to meet Melissa Freedman and her parents.'

Kathryn knew this meant a lot to Jack. 'I'd be delighted.' As she followed him out of his office his secretary gave her the thumbs-up—without Jack seeing, of course. At least she'd been successful in getting Jack out of his bad mood.

Kathryn had thought she was prepared to meet Melissa, but when they walked to her bed she faltered at the sight of the small child beneath the white hospital sheets. Immediately she pasted on a smile for the parents.

'Just thought I'd stop by, before going home,' Jack said to Melissa's parents. 'I'd like to introduce you to a friend of mine. Rebekah and Alan Freedman, this is Kathryn Pearce.'

Kathryn shook their hands and murmured a greeting.

'Are you a specialist?' Rebekah asked. 'I'm sure I've seen you around the hospital.'

Kathryn nodded. 'I'm an orthopaedic surgeon.'

'Oh. Do you need to look at her skull or something to make sure it's healing?' Rebekah asked in puzzlement.

'No. I'm not here in a medical capacity. I'm a good friend of Jack's and he wanted me to meet you and Melissa because she's a special patient of his.'

'So this is the love of your life,' Alan joked to Jack. 'Well done. Quite a catch.'

'She's not a fish, darling,' Rebekah told her husband, but the smile on her face belied the seriousness of her words.

Kathryn looked down at Melissa who was lying still, hooked up to all kinds of machines. Jack asked her parents a few questions about her progress, but Kathryn's eyes were glued to the hauntingly beautiful little girl.

Her blonde hair had been brushed up into a ponytail on top of her head and was held in place with a bright red satin ribbon. Around the base of her skull was a white pressure bandage which hid the wound and the hair that had been shaved from her head.

Her eyes were open and glassy as she stared into space, only her right eye was turned in. Her arms were resting outside the sheets, the fingers on her right hand twisted in paralysis. Her mouth, on the right side, was dribbling, and Kathryn reached for a tissue and gently wiped her lips.

'The physiotherapist is happy with her progress. Every day Melissa manages to comprehend a little bit more,' Rebekah said as she leaned over and kissed her daughter's cheek. 'We're all quite determined to get through this. We know it will take time but we still have our daughter and that's all that counts.'

'Congratulations,' Kathryn said, her voice soft. 'Melissa *will* recover because of the love and support you'll be giving her.'

'We also have the support of our extended families,' Alan said, and placed his arm about his wife's shoulders. 'Through them we'll receive the help that *we* need. Someone to babysit Melissa while we get out of the house and take a break.'

'Very important,' Kathryn replied. 'I hope you've been reassured that the medical and nursing staff of this hospital are here to assist.'

'Jack's drummed that into us from the very beginning.' Rebekah smiled at Jack who shrugged nonchalantly. 'The past few months have been horrendous for everyone, especially Melissa, but the worst is over and from now the only way is up.'

The physiotherapist joined them at Melissa's bedside, announcing it was time for her evening session of physio. Jack and Kathryn excused themselves and walked out of ICU.

'Coffee?' Jack asked, and at her nod he steered her toward the cafeteria. When they were seated, with steaming mugs of coffee before them, Kathryn cleared her throat.

'She's one lucky girl. Those parents of hers love her so unconditionally.'

'Most parents do.' Jack sipped his coffee.

'I guess it's because we see more of the child abuse cases, the abandonments, the babies that are born deformed or have a mental disability than the rest of society. So when I meet people like the Floringtons, Abigail Brooks and now the Freedmans I'm pleasantly surprised to see that they would go to the ends of the earth for their children.'

'I know what you mean.' Jack reached out his hand and covered hers. 'You love children, don't you?' It was a statement more than a question. 'I know that most professionals in the paediatric business get on well with kids but you really *care* and *love* these children.'

'So do you,' Kathryn whispered, and squeezed his hand.

'You'll make a wonderful mother, Katy.'

Emotion rose in her throat to form a big lump, and she could feel the tears pricking at her eyes. She looked down at their entwined fingers and then looked back into his eyes.

'Thank you.' It was all she could say.

Jack and Kathryn managed to meet for a twenty-minute lunch the following day. Kathryn had a busy all-day theatre list and Jack was in clinic. On Friday they missed each other completely and she cursed their differing schedules.

Prudence Florington, along with Penelope and Sally, came into the clinic for her two-week review.

'You've been a very good girl,' Kathryn told her, and gave both the girls a lolly, after getting the nod from their mother. Prudence had been wearing the walking splint for the past two weeks and, from Kathryn's examination, all was healed and well.

'She's been annoyed with it the last few days and hasn't wanted to wear it during the day. At night-time she's more than happy to have it on.' Sally rolled her eyes. 'But I persisted and told her Dr Kathryn would take it off for her.'

'Which I have. You and Gregory have done a wonderful job with her.' Kathryn was full of praise. 'Parental attitudes make all the difference.'

'So does good medical treatment and good nursing. Once we're finished here we'll pop around to the ward and see the nurses. Now, let's make a date to have you and Jack over for dinner.'

When Kathryn didn't protest Sally smiled. 'Worked things out, have you?'

'Not quite.' Kathryn relented. 'How does four weeks from Friday sound? I know Jack's free because he leaves the following day for a conference overseas.'

'Great. We'll look forward to having you. If you can make it around seven you'll be able to see the girls before they go to bed.'

'We wouldn't miss it for the world.'

That evening, after she'd eaten dinner with Steven and put the dishes into the dishwasher, the doorbell rang. 'I'll go,' Steven said, and returned a few minutes later with an enormous bunch of spring flowers.

'Have you finally asked that registrar out? And did she like you *that* much?' Kathryn joked, and her brother pulled a face.

'They're for you, silly. Jack must have really done something wrong to send you a bunch this big. And, yes, for your information, I have asked *that* registrar out. We had a great time. Perhaps we can all double date some time.' He broke into a fit of laughter at his own suggestion. 'Oh, yeah... I can just see her relaxing, with the professor sitting opposite her.'

Kathryn took the flowers and read the card.

You requested flowers eight weeks ago and I just found the memo. Hope you enjoy them. I miss you.

Kathryn's eyes misted over with tears as she searched for some vases. She didn't have one big enough to hold the whole bunch so she spent the next half-hour arranging and rearranging the flowers around the house.

'Phew,' Steven said, holding his nose. 'Smells like a florist's shop in here.'

'If you don't like it then go away,' Kathryn said as she tenderly touched the petal of a pale pink rose.

'You're getting soppy in your old age, Kath.'

The next morning she called Jack and thanked him for the flowers. They both had a few hours to spare and arranged to meet at the archery park. The game was a hoot and Kathryn knew she'd never been happier in her life.

Over the next four weeks they spent as much time together as their workloads would allow. The subject of her sister was still lurking in the back of her mind, and Kathryn knew her relationship with Jack could only progress so far before that talk would be necessary. Until they got to that point she was going to enjoy herself.

Joel Brooks was finally discharged after six weeks. Kathryn had removed his external fixator, but the plates and screws in his arm would need to stay in for a while longer. His shunt was working perfectly and Jack was immensely pleased with his progress.

Abigail and her husband both had their plaster casts removed, and although they still needed extensive physiotherapy they were much better than before.

'You and your staff have done so much,' Abigail said to Jack and Kathryn as the family prepared to go home. 'The effort, the care and love you've all shown will be with us always.'

'Just make sure you bring him back for a visit,' Joan said. 'We like to see our patients when they're fit and healthy. It lifts our morale.'

'We will,' Abigail promised. Joel had review appointments in both Jack's and Kathryn's clinics so they'd be seeing the family in a few weeks' time.

On Friday Kathryn picked out a russet red floral dress. The weather had begun to warm up, though the evenings were still quite cool. Reaching for a cream cardigan, she waited for Jack to collect her.

When he arrived he scooped her into his arms and gave her a passionate kiss. 'I was thinking about you all day long.'

'The whole day?' Kathryn asked disbelievingly, and he nodded. 'If you say so.'

'What time do we have to be there?'

'Sally said around seven. It's now six-thirty so we'd better get going.'

'Where are the presents for the girls?'

'Thanks. I nearly forgot.' Kathryn retraced her steps to her room and collected two large bags which held wrapped presents for Prudence and Penelope. She and Jack had discussed in detail what to buy for the two little girls who had captured their hearts, and had decided on a children's medical kit for each.

'They're going to love those stethoscopes,' Kathryn said as Jack helped her into the Jaguar.

'It's their toys I feel sorry for,' Jack said with a laugh.

They enjoyed a wonderful evening, relaxing with the Floringtons. Friendships with patients and their families were part of a doctor's reward. It was past midnight when Jack walked Kathryn to her door.

'Want to come in for a coffee?'

'I've drunk enough coffee,' he replied, his eyes gleaming with desire, 'but I'll come in anyway.'

Nevertheless, Kathryn put the kettle on and checked Steven's room. He wasn't home. They snuggled on the couch and reflected on the evening.

'I can see us with a pair of mischief-makers like those two little darlings,' Jack said, and Kathryn turned to look at him.

'Can you really?' Her heart hammered in her chest. It was the first reference to a future that Jack had made. A future that included her.

'Seeing Gregory and Sally so happy makes me believe there are happy endings out there for us all. We just have to reach up and take hold.' He looked at her intensely. 'I love you, Katy.'

'I love you too,' Kathryn replied, and kissed him with passion. After a while Jack broke free and gazed down upon her face.

'Amazing, isn't it? I never thought lightning struck twice but apparently it does.' It was as though he were talking to himself, and his words made Kathryn stiffen. Feeling her withdrawal, Jack held her tighter. 'Don't take that the wrong way, Kathryn. You know what I mean.'

'Do I, Jack? Do I?' She struggled free of his grasp. 'How can I possibly know what you mean when you won't tell me what happened?'

His jaw clenched, then relaxed as he tried to hold on to his temper. 'I loved Jill. Past tense.'

'But that's only because she died. Didn't you ever wonder what would have happened if she'd lived? You'd probably have been my brother-in-law for the past ten years.' Kathryn stood and glared down at him.

'Whether Jill had lived or not is irrelevant. I'm a different person now to who I was then. I have different morals, a different outlook on life.'

'How am I supposed to know that? I didn't *know* you back then.' Her voice rose another decibel and she could feel the panic begin to take a firm grip around her heart.

'I'll tell you what I was like, shall I? I was selfish and hypocritical. I wanted to go and help in Third World countries not because I cared about the people but because it looked good on a résumé. Even when I got there I failed to be touched by the misery and poverty those people called life. I didn't like myself one bit.'

'So what changed you? Or should I ask who?'

'I—won't—discuss—it.' He said each word as though it were a death sentence. 'I don't understand why you can't accept the fact that I don't want to relive my past. I don't want to remember the person I was. I've changed dramatically and actually like the person I am today.' He got to his feet. 'If you can't accept me as I am now, regardless of what happened in my past, then there's nothing more to say.'

'It's not *your* past that I care about, Jack. It's Jill's. Can't *you* understand, I *need* to know what happened to her. She was my sister. My own flesh and blood, and I loved her too.' Kathryn was in full temper now and tears were streaming down her face.

'I grieve for her every day and I wonder what on earth went so wrong that the entire village was massacred. It's so surreal. You *know*, Jack. You *can* help me but you *won't*. If you loved me you wouldn't put me through this pain.'

'Ditto,' he replied, and reached into his pocket for his keys. 'I can tell you one thing. I would never have become your brother-in-law. If Jill had lived I never would have married her.'

'Why not?' Kathryn asked, her voice shaky and filled with emotion.

'Because she wasn't in love with me.' With that, he turned and walked out the door. Out of her life.

Kathryn's alarm buzzed at five o'clock the next morning. She reached out and flicked it off as she felt a new bout of tears begin to flow. She was supposed to take Jack to the airport this morning, but after what had happened last night there was no way she was going to face him so soon.

His parting words had echoed around her head for most of the night. Jill hadn't loved him. He'd loved Jill but her sister hadn't returned his love and affection, and Kathryn wondered why. Jack was such a strong and caring man. His attitude toward his staff and his patients was commendable.

But he'd also said he'd changed considerably from the person he'd been ten years ago. Perhaps if Jill had been alive today they might have been together. She shook her head and reached for another tissue. There was no point in surmising what would or wouldn't have happened. Jill was dead.

Her death had changed Kathryn and it had changed Jack, but she still couldn't help feeling a little jealous about the relationship the man she loved had enjoyed with her sister. That they had been good friends was undoubtable, but Jack's parting words had made Kathryn think.

Jill hadn't loved him—but Kathryn did. More than anything in the world, Kathryn loved him with all her heart and soul. She needed Jack to be a part of her life, but a marriage needed to be built on the solid foundation of trust—and Jack didn't trust her.

She blew her nose and threw the tissue in the direction of the bin. It landed on the floor with the others that had missed. She turned over and closed her eyes. The images of Jack, walking out the door, returned and Kathryn flung the covers back and went into the kitchen.

She made herself a cup of chamomile tea and sat at the kitchen table, sipping it. Her life seemed empty and hopeless. She wanted to cry but her eyes were already too puffy, her head ached and all the tears had been wrung out. Feeling her eyes begin to droop, Kathryn padded back to bed and slept until mid-afternoon.

She wallowed in her misery all Sunday. When Steven gently probed, she informed him that Jack wouldn't be coming back—at least not to her. It was over. Thankfully, her brother didn't press the issue and left her alone to watch old movies.

On Monday she arrived at work, still feeling like death warmed up. When Kathryn had seen the last patient from her morning clinic, there was a knock at her door. She looked up to see a man in his late forties, with brown hair, greying slightly at the temples. She hadn't approved another patient but she forced a smile nevertheless.

'Can I help you?'

He took his hands out of his pockets and walked across to her. 'I'm Tim Conway.'

The smile almost slipped but, instead, she stood and accepted his outstretched hand.

'Welcome back. Please, have a seat.'

'Thanks,' Tim nodded. 'I was hoping to catch Jack but his secretary told me he's overseas this week.' As he sat down he handed Kathryn some papers. 'It's a psychological evaluation, clearing me for work.'

Kathryn felt a lump rise in her throat and she quickly scanned the papers. She swallowed the lump and smiled. 'It's your job, Tim. I'm just keeping the chair warm.'

'Thanks, Kathryn. I appreciate it. You have the legal right to continue in the position for the next three months and I won't contest it.' He stood and walked around the room with his hands in his pockets. 'Up until Connie's death I was so busy, caring for her. Then there was the funeral to organise and the memorial service. Now...I feel at a loose end. I need to work, Kathryn. I need to fill my time, and caring for my patients seems the most logical thing to do.'

'I understand,' Kathryn replied and stood. 'We can make this week a hand-over week. I've really enjoyed myself but I think it's time to move on.'

She'd felt a sense of doom when Tim had walked into the room, but during his speech she realised that an escape from Jack was just what she needed. Tim was giving her a way out, and if she timed everything well she could leave Adelaide before Jack returned from his overseas conference.

When she went to her office—Tim's office, she corrected herself—she made a few phone calls to Melbourne. Half an hour later she had a locum position at her old hospital set up to begin the following Monday. She called the airline and booked a one-way ticket, departing on Friday evening.

Persuading herself that she was doing the right thing, Kathryn grabbed a quick bite and went to Theatre. After her list she bumped into Joan, who, by the stern look on her face, had heard the latest news.

'You can't leave, Kathryn,' she said. 'You have a contract with the hospital to stay for six months. I know Tim is lonely after Connie's death but that's no excuse to go pushing you out of the way. Why doesn't he take a holiday overseas and enjoy himself?'

'That's irrelevant, Joan. If both the hospital and I are willing to reach an amicable arrangement to break the contract then it can be done without any legal implications. I've lined up another job at my old hospital and booked my ticket.'

'Have you spoken to Jack? He'll be furious if he comes back and finds you gone.'

'None of this concerns Jack.'

'Rubbish,' Joan snorted. 'You're perfect for each other. What's wrong? Did you have another little fight?'

'There are circumstances you couldn't possibly understand, Joan.'

'Try me.'

Kathryn shook her head. 'It's between Jack and myself. To tell you the truth, I sincerely doubt he'll be furious when he comes back and finds me gone. He'll probably congratulate himself on a lucky escape and be back to dating bimbos in no time at all.'

'Must have been a good fight,' Joan said, 'but it can be fixed. Anything can be fixed if you're willing to do some mending.'

'Not this time, Joan,' Kathryn said softly, and gave her friend a watery smile. 'It's back to Melbourne for me.'

Joan wasn't the only one who tried to talk her out of going. Steven came down like a ton of bricks.

'What about Jack?' he protested on Thursday evening as Kathryn packed her bags.

'I told you before, Steven, it's over. Tim's return has only speeded the process. Instead of having to spend the next three months enduring hospital gossip, difficult meetings and a cold stony silence from Jack, I can return to my old hospital and pick up the pieces of my life.'

'Do you love him?' Steven asked softly.

'Yes, but there's more to a relationship than love, Steven. I once thought it was enough, but it isn't.'

'What is it? Why can't you tell me?'

'It's personal.' There was no way Kathryn was going to subject Steven to the same pain she was going through at Jack's reticence to talk about Jill. Once Jack had told Kathryn, she would break the news to her family so they, too, could achieve closure. Anything had to be better than the emptiness she'd carried around for the past ten years.

'Look on the bright side, Steven,' she said. She reached for the keys to the Mazda and tossed them to him.

'What? The Mazda? I can keep it?'

'For the time being,' she smiled. 'Mum and Dad's car is still at my place so I'll use that.'

'Thanks, Kath.' He kissed her and left her to pack.

Friday was a mixture of sadness and relief as she said goodbye to the ward staff, theatre staff and everyone in between. One special stop she had to make was to see Melissa Freedman and her parents.

In the past few weeks she had often dropped by, and had been astounded at Melissa's progress. It was late in the day and she tapped on the door, before walking in. Rebekah stopped in mid-sentence in the book she was reading to her daughter. A smile made its way across Kathryn's face as she looked at the sweet girl in the bed.

'You're sitting up!' she said to Melissa, and gave a little clap.

'Well done.' Her enthusiasm made Melissa's crooked mouth curve into what could only be called a smile. A little lopsided but still a smile.

'This is the new breakthrough,' Rebekah said as she put down the book. 'Everyone is so ecstatic.'

'As you should be,' Kathryn said as she walked over to the bedside. She grasped Melissa's left hand and gave it a squeeze. 'You're a very clever girl. Is Daddy at work?' There was understanding in her eyes and Kathryn could see the struggle the child was having to answer.

'Yes,' Rebekah said. 'Daddy's at work but he'll be back soon. What a surprise he will get when he sees his clever girl sitting up in bed.' Rebekah kissed her daughter and handed her the book. She could use her left hand to turn the pages—another good sign.

'It's been five weeks now,' Rebekah said in hushed tones. 'We can't believe how wonderfully she's progressed. She tires easily, of course, but everyone says that's to be expected.'

'It is. Sooner than you think, she'll be under your feet again.'

'How I long for that day,' Rebekah said on a sigh. 'She's missed Dr Jack this week. When is he back?'

Kathryn looked down at her hands and then back to Rebekah. 'On Sunday.'

'Good. Are you looking forward to his return?'

'Yes and no,' Kathryn said with forced enthusiasm. 'I'm actually leaving this evening for Melbourne.'

'Oh, what a pity. You'll miss each other. When do you return?'

'Not for another six months at least. I have a new position there that begins on Monday.'

'Really?' Rebekah was quite astounded. 'So you leave tonight?'

'Yes. I stopped by to see how Melissa was progressing and to say goodbye. It's been a very emotional day, saying farewell to everyone, but Melissa has managed to make me very happy, seeing her sitting up. You and Alan are doing a marvellous job with her. She's a credit to you both.'

'Thank you, Kathryn.' Rebekah held out her hand. 'I'll wish you all the best and perhaps, if you're ever back in Adelaide, you'll take the opportunity to look us up?'

'I'd be delighted.' Kathryn shook her hand and then reached down and gave Melissa's hand another squeeze. 'Dr Kathryn has to go away, Melissa, but you keep on getting better. Dr Jack will be around in a few days to see you.'

There was another smile at the mention of Jack's name. Kathryn's heart felt heavy. She had to get out of here before she burst into tears.

'Take care,' she whispered, before leaving the room.

She had managed to pull off the great escape, she thought as she sat in her aisle seat on the aeroplane. If Jack's secretary or anyone else had sent him word of her departure, he obviously didn't care enough to stop her. Telling Joan the contract had nothing to do with Jack wasn't completely true. One word from Jack, whether in person or by way of an overseas fax, would have effectively stopped her departure. It hadn't happened.

With no one to meet her at Tullamarine airport in Melbourne, Kathryn took a taxi to her inner city unit which she shared with one of her colleagues. Andrea was rushing out the door as Kathryn arrived.

'Sorry I can't stay and chat. I've been called in to assist with quads. Oh, the life of a paediatrician is never dull,' she said with a laugh as she closed the door behind her.

Kathryn let the silence envelop her, before dragging her suitcases off to her room. Throwing herself onto the bed, which Andrea had kindly made up for her, she gave way to tears.

By Monday she'd pulled herself together and was negotiating Melbourne traffic in her parents' Range Rover. Kathryn parked the car and reported for duty. She spent the morning catching up with old friends and making some new ones.

In the evening, her pager beeped and she rang the switchboard.

'I've got a Professor Holden on the line for you. He left some messages earlier with the orthopaedic department secretary, but as you haven't called him back he's presuming you didn't get them.'

'I did,' Kathryn confessed to Maude, who was one of the hospital's longest-serving switchboard operators. 'I was ignoring him. Did he sound mad?'

'Not at all,' Maude confessed. 'He sounds like a darling. Very polite and charming. Is he good-looking?'

'Yes.' Kathryn sighed and knew it was inevitable that she spoke to him. 'Put him through, Maude, thank you.' She waited for the click before saying, 'What's the problem, Jack?'

'As if you didn't know, Kathryn.'

The sound of his voice was as smooth as silk and she felt her knees go weak. Slumping into a chair, she closed her eyes and tried to control her breathing. Maude had been wrong. Kathryn could tell from those few words that he was mad. In fact, he wasn't just mad, he was spitting chips!

'Why did you do it?'

'Tim needed his job back so I stepped aside.'

'You didn't need to and you know it. How do you think it made me look when I return from overseas to discover the orthopaedic department has changed directors. Considering I'm supposed to know what's happening with all surgical departments, it made me look like an incompetent fool.'

Is that all he cared about? Looking like a fool? Angry tears misted her eyes and she tried to control the urge not to slam the phone down in his ear.

'Sorry,' she snapped. 'Forgive me if I've made you look a fool. I can promise you it will never happen again.'

'Damn it, woman! Why do you take everything the wrong way?' he roared. 'When I returned from overseas yesterday morning I called your home to try and work things out. Imagine my surprise when Steven tells me you've returned to Melbourne—permanently.'

'It seemed like the right thing to do,' she replied. 'We're at an impasse, Jack. You refuse to talk about Jill and that indicates you don't trust me.'

'Trust! That's a laugh, coming from you. Why can't you trust me? Did you once stop to think that talking about my life in Africa could be painful for me? Why can't you accept me for who I am?'

Their tempers were both in full swing, and Kathryn was sure that had they been facing each other objects would have been thrown. Perhaps it was just as well that all this was being said over the phone.

'There's nothing more to say, Jack. I left Adelaide to save us both the heartache of having to work with each other day in day out for the next three months.'

'Heartache! You don't know the meaning of the word because you don't have one,' he snarled. 'You said you loved me. Well, this is a rotten way to show it, Kathryn.'

'The same could be said of you,' she retorted, the tears flowing down her cheeks. 'You're still hung up on the fact that Jill didn't love you. I do love you, Jack, but I need you to let go of her. Do you have any idea how it makes me feel? I feel like second choice. I always had to live up to Jill's reputation during med school and I don't see why I should now have to tolerate it in my own love life. Let go of her, Jack.'

'You're the one who needs to let go, Kathryn.'

'I *can't* until *you* tell me what *happened*!' Kathryn almost screamed the words down the phone. 'You need to trust me, Jack, and until you can we have nothing further to say to each other.' This time she *did* slam down the phone. Severing the connection between them.

The next few weeks were the loneliest of Kathryn's life. She went through the motions of living but didn't enjoy life. Patients came and went with the days. Stores were full of Christmas cheer and hospital celebrations were being organised in every department. None of this made a difference to her.

Every Monday afternoon the department of surgery had its weekly meeting. All staff were required to attend, from the highest-paid consultant to interns and medical students. Generally the turn-out was nearly one hundred people.

After Kathryn had arrived and taken a seat, they were informed that the agenda for the meeting had been changed as an interstate visiting dignitary was going to address them.

'Want to try sneaking out the door?' Brian, one of her orthopaedic colleagues, whispered in her ear.

She turned to smile at him and whispered, 'We're too close to the front. They'll catch us.' They grinned at each other before she gave her attention to the guest speaker.

Her body flushed hot then cold, and for a moment Kathryn thought she was going to faint. Professor Jack Holden stood at the podium, dressed in a navy suit, arranging his overhead transparencies. Her palms began to sweat and a tingle of apprehension fizzled through her. What was he doing here? Why hadn't she known he was coming?

'My name,' he said into the microphone, 'is Professor Jack Holden. Today, among other things, I would like to discuss a new surgical technique in the area of dermoid tumours.' With that, he proceeded to give his presentation.

Kathryn found it difficult to sit in her chair and listen. Why was he here? Had he missed her? Why did he have to look so handsome? Why did her heart have to pound so much at the mere sight of him? Slowly, as he continued speaking, she began to focus on his words and soon found herself listening attentively to his teaching.

After his conclusion there was a brief round of applause, but he held up his hands for silence. 'There is one other issue I'd like to raise while I have the opportunity.'

Alarm bells began to ring inside Kathryn's head but she remained glued to her seat.

'I'd like to point out the advantages and disadvantages of strategic retreat.'

There were a few puzzled murmurs and glances as they wondered what he was talking about. Kathryn knew exactly where his words were directed. At her.

'Could we have the lights dimmed, please?' He waited for this to happen before the overhead projector illuminated his first transparency. 'My first overhead shows when not to make a strategic retreat. If the situation becomes unmanageable or too hard to handle, it is generally the wrong time to pull away.'

'As you can see here, it is better to take charge of the situation to alleviate the problems.'

People in the auditorium were now completely perplexed by the mumbo-jumbo the visiting professor was spouting.

'That's why,' Jack continued, 'I like to take charge of situations.' He changed the overhead to one that read in big, black letters, KATHRYN PEARCE. I LOVE YOU AND I TRUST YOU. MARRY ME.

A roar spread through the room as a few people slapped Kathryn on the back, urging her to go up to the front. All Kathryn wanted to do was sink as low as possible in her chair. Unfortunately, the ground refused to open up and swallow her so she allowed herself to be cajoled and walked on wobbly legs to the front.

Jack reached for her hand and said into the microphone, 'Now, if you'll excuse us, we have some unfinished business to discuss. Thank you for your time and co-operation.'

The house lights came up as Jack dragged Kathryn from the room. A few of the students and interns clapped and wolf-whistled but all this was hazy in Kathryn's mind.

Jack was here. Jack had come for her. Jack loved her *and* trusted her.

He pulled her into a back office and switched on the light, before closing and locking the door. They stood looking at each other for a moment before Jack gathered her into his arms and pressed his lips hungrily against hers. Neither of them spoke for the next few minutes as they intimately re-acquainted themselves.

'Please sit down,' he said, and held her at arm's length. 'There are a few things I need to say to you before we can allow our passion to run its course.' He grinned and gave her one final kiss, then took a few steps back. Kathryn sat, thankful she was no longer required to support herself.

'Surprised to see me?' he asked, and she nodded. 'Can you speak at all?'

Kathryn opened her mouth, then closed it again and shook her head. 'That's a first,' he joked, and she managed a smile.

'You were right, Kathryn. I didn't trust you. The past few weeks have been murder without you and it made me realise you need to know about my life in Africa and about Jill before we can go forward and enjoy *our* life together. It was trying to survive without you that finally drummed it into me. Our marriage needs to have a solid foundation so it's time to clear away the rubbish.'

'You're so arrogant, Jack Holden,' she said, with love in her eyes. 'I haven't said yes yet.'

'You will,' he insisted. Unable to keep his hands off her, Jack kissed her—until she whispered the one word he needed to hear. 'See,' he said conceitedly. 'I knew you'd agree.'

Kathryn rolled her eyes and smiled.

'I have another surprise for you,' he said.

'After the last one, I'm afraid to ask.'

'How does the position of Director of Orthopaedics in Adelaide sound?'

Kathryn's eyes widened in delight. 'But what about Tim Conway?'

'He's resigned. He realised it was too soon to return to work. He's already left to go overseas and visit some of his old friends. So the job is yours—if you can stand working closely with your husband, that is.'

'How close?' she asked, and gave him a seductive wink.

'Closer than you've ever imagined,' he replied, and they both smiled. 'But first...' the smile slid from his face as he stood before her '...I must tell you about Africa.' He closed his eyes for a moment and took a breath.

'Jack...' Kathryn had never seen him so tormented and wished she could spare him the pain, but she knew they needed to clear away the past.

'No, please. Don't interrupt me. It's a long and painful story but it must be told.' He took a deep breath and looked directly into Kathryn's honey brown eyes.

'Jill and I, along with some other friends, went across to Africa to offer our assistance to the unfortunate people who so desperately needed medical attention. As I told you previously, I did it for the recognition to get myself a better job. I was so selfish back then.' The self-disgust was evident in his voice. 'I know I've changed for the better but, then, tragedy has a way of changing us all.

'We'd been in a village for nearly two months when a wedding was announced. We were all invited to join in the festivities. Weddings are a very big deal and the celebrations usually last for several days.

'Everyone rejoices and takes the opportunity to forget about the day-to-day problems surrounding them. Alcohol is consumed in vast amounts and, let me tell you, the alcohol those people make is one hundred per cent proof. We were *all* drinking, as it was bad manners not to toast the bride and groom every ten minutes.

'At the end of the first day of celebrations the entire village was in a drunken stupor. After the newlyweds had finally retired to their hut the numbers began to dwindle. Most of the people wanted to sleep off the effects of the alcohol in readiness for the following day's festivities. Some of the men were going off to the still where they brew the alcohol to keep celebrating through the night and into the next morning. The groom's father was amongst them. With a little bit of coaxing, I gave in and joined them.'

His eyes glazed over and he looked beyond Kathryn. She noticed the pain and anguish reflected in his face but didn't dare make a move to comfort him. She needed to know.

'If only I hadn't...' His voice trailed off before he continued in a bleak tone, 'I tried to persuade Jill to come with me but she refused. She was tired and wanted to go to bed. So I went with the men and we continued to drink.

'They came out of nowhere. Guerrillas. Because we were just out of the village and also very intoxicated, we weren't even sure what was happening. We could hear the loud bangs from the guns and, as though in slow motion, we scrambled our way back to the village. It was too late. They'd been into each hut and just let the bullets fly. The devastation was...' Jack closed his eyes, trying to block out the images.

'The other men who were with me were sobbing with loss. I felt nothing but disgust. Disgust with myself. If I hadn't gone to the still I could have done something to stop this disaster from happening. I don't know what I would have done but it would have been better than drinking myself unconscious.

'I heard another crack split the air and turned around. I was face to face with one of the murderers. I froze. Anger and hatred mixed together as I looked into his eyes. He had the audacity to smile—his white teeth were like a flash of light in the dark, bleak night. He was enjoying himself. I couldn't hold back any longer and charged at him with complete hatred. I heard him laugh as his finger pulled back on the trigger and let the bullets spray into me. I felt them hit my leg and chest. I fell to the ground, unable to move. Then I passed out.'

Kathryn's tears were silently streaming down her face and Jack lifted his clean, white handkerchief to wipe them away. He pulled over a chair and sat down beside her. They stared at each other for a long moment before he continued quietly, 'The next set of events are a blur but, from what I was told, some people from a neighbouring village had arrived on a visit, as they often did. They were the ones who found the devastation. They searched for survivors and found three. Two other villagers and myself. Everyone else was dead—including Jill.

'Getting us medical attention wasn't easy and they carried us for two days to the nearest hospital. The bullet was removed from my leg and the one that hit my chest miraculously missed every vital organ. The other two villagers died shortly after we arrived at the hospital. I stayed there for almost a year, allowing my physical and emotional scars to heal. I was the sole survivor.'

He shook his head sadly. 'Jill. I never told her I loved her. I knew she didn't feel the same way about me. We were close friends and she was always telling me to stop thinking about myself. To give to others—those in need. To use my skill to heal people, not to exploit them for monetary gain.

'I now know that what I felt for Jill was not true love. It's you and only you, Katy. With you I feel complete. I *never* felt that way with Jill. I love you.' The last three words were said quietly but with such heartfelt urgency that Kathryn pressed her lips against his, reciprocating the emotion.

The salty taste of Kathryn's tears mingled in their mouths as they passionately embraced. 'Jack.' Kathryn breathed his name and continued kissing away his hurt. Finally, they broke apart and she rested her head on his shoulder. 'Thank you. I don't know what else to say, Jack, except thank you. The fact that you've shared this with me makes me love you all the more.' He held her tightly, and for quite a while they sat in silence.

Kathryn raised her head and gazed up at him. He gave her a small smile. 'You look as vulnerable as you did that day on the ski slopes.'

'It seems such a long time ago,' she murmured, feeling all the tension inside her being released.

'How about we go there for our honeymoon? I'll give you personalised skiing lessons.' He gave her a wicked grin and raised his eyebrows suggestively.

'Ah, no. I don't think that's such a good idea,' she countered, remembering Lyn's waspish warning to stay away from the handsome doctor. 'However, I wouldn't mind sailing the Whitsundays with you. Think about it. Just the two of us—no emergencies—no phones—no people.'

'Sounds fantastic,' he smiled. 'When do we leave?'

'After the wedding, Jack.'

'Oh, right.' He chuckled. 'I'd forgotten.' He looked at her with love in his eyes. 'Did you like my method of proposal?'

Kathryn shook her head as she recalled her earlier embarrassment. 'I don't believe you did it but, boy, am I glad you did. We've been locked in this room for so long I can just imagine what people think we're doing.'

'Why should we disappoint them?' Jack grinned wickedly at her and gathered her closer.

MILLS & BOON®

*M*akes
any time
special

Enjoy a romantic novel from
Mills & Boon®

Presents™ *Enchanted*™ *Temptation*™

Historical Romance™ *Medical Romance*™

MILLS & BOON®

Medical Romance™

COMING NEXT MONTH

VALENTINE MAGIC by Margaret Barker

Dr Tim Fielding found it impossible to believe that Katie didn't want a relationship, but she was determined to remain independent and *definitely* single!

THE FAMILY TOUCH by Sheila Danton

The attraction between Callum Smith and Fran Bergmont was potent, but as a very new single mother, she needed time before risking involvement again.

THE BABY AFFAIR by Marion Lennox

Jock Blaxton adored every baby he delivered, so why didn't he have his own? Having his baby wasn't a problem for Tina Rafter, but Jock?

A COUNTRY CALLING by Leah Martyn

A&E wasn't easy, and dealing with Nick Cavallo was no picnic either for Melanie Stewart, so it surprised her when they became friends—and more?

Available from 5th February 1999

Available at most branches of WH Smith, Tesco, Asda, Martins, Borders, Easons, Volume One/James Thin and most good paperback bookshops

ELIZABETH GAGE

When Dusty brings home her young fiancé, he is everything her mother Rebecca Lowell could wish for her daughter, *and for herself...*

The Lowell family's descent into darkness begins with one bold act, one sin committed in an otherwise blameless life. This time there's no absolution in...

Confession

He's a cop, she's his prime suspect

MARY LYNN
BAXTER

HARD
CANDY

He's crossed the line no cop ever should.
He's involved with a suspect—his
prime suspect.

Falling for the wrong man is far down her
list of troubles.

Until he arrests her for murder.

 Available from 18th December 1998

books and a surprise gift!

We would like to take this opportunity to thank you for reading this Mills & Boon® book by offering you the chance to take TWO more specially selected titles from the Medical Romance™ series absolutely FREE! We're also making this offer to introduce you to the benefits of the Reader Service™—

- ★ FREE home delivery
- ★ FREE gifts and competitions
- ★ FREE monthly Newsletter
- ★ Books available before they're in the shops
- ★ Exclusive Reader Service discounts

Accepting these FREE books and gift places you under no obligation to buy, you may cancel at any time, even after receiving your free shipment. Simply complete your details below and return the entire page to the address below. *You don't even need a stamp!*

YES! Please send me 2 free Medical Romance books and a surprise gift. I understand that unless you hear from me, I will receive 4 superb new titles every month for just £2.30 each, postage and packing free. I am under no obligation to purchase any books and may cancel my subscription at any time. The free books and gift will be mine to keep in any case.

M9EA

Ms/Mrs/Miss/Mr ....Initials ....
BLOCK CAPITALS PLEASE

Surname ....

Address ....

....

....Postcode...............................

Send this whole page to:
THE READER SERVICE, FREEPOST CN81, CROYDON, CR9 3WZ
(Eire readers please send coupon to: P.O. Box 4546, DUBLIN 24.)

Offer not valid to current Reader Service subscribers to this series. We reserve the right to refuse an application and applicants must be aged 18 years or over. Only one application per household. Terms and prices subject to change without notice. Offer expires 31st July 1999. As a result of this application, you may receive further offers from Harlequin Mills & Boon and other carefully selected companies. If you would prefer not to share in this opportunity please write to The Data Manager at the address above.

Medical Romance is being used as a trademark.

JOANN ROSS

a woman's heart

In *A Woman's Heart*, JoAnn Ross has created a rich, lyrical love story about land, community, family and the very special bond between a man who doesn't believe in anything and a woman who believes in him.

MIRA®   **Available from February**